WAR AND PEACE

BOOK FIFTEEN : 1812 - 13

By Leo Tolstoy

Double9 BOOKS

War and Peace Book 15
by Leo Tolstoy

ISBN: 978-93-94973-64-0

Published by
DOUBLE 9 BOOKS
2/13-B, Ansari Road
Daryaganj, New Delhi - 110002
info@double9books.com
www.double9books.com
Tel. 011-40042856

Printed in India.

About the Author

Leo Tolstoy was a Russian creator known for his books War and Peace which is viewed as the best book of pragmatist fiction. Tolstoy is additionally viewed as world's best author by quite a few people. Additionally an ethical scholar and a social reformer, Tolstoy had extreme moralistic points of view. In later life, he turned into an intense Christian rebel and anarcho-conservative.

Leo Tolstoy Born in Yasnaya Polyana on September 9, 1828, He had a place with a notable honorable Russian family. He was the fourth among five offspring of Count Nikolai Ilyich Tolstoy and Countess Mariya Tolstaya, both of whom kicked the bucket passing on their youngsters to be raised by family members.

In 1844, Tolstoy was acknowledged into Kazan University. Incapable to graduate past the subsequent year, Tolstoy got back to Yasnava Polyana and afterward invested energy going among Moscow and St. Petersburg. With some functioning information on a few dialects, he turned into a multilingual. Yet again the recently observed youth pulled in Tolstoy towards drinking, visiting massage parlors and most betting which left him in weighty obligation and anguish however Tolstoy before long acknowledged he was carrying on with a brutish life and endeavored college tests with the expectation that he would acquire a situation with the public authority, yet finished yet up in Caucuses serving in the military continuing in the strides of his senior sibling.

In Year 1862, Leo Tolstoy wedded Sophia Andreevna Behrs, generally called Sonya, who was 16 years more youthful than him. The couple had thirteen youngsters, of which, five passed on at an early age. Sonya went about as Tolstoy's secretary, editor and monetary chief while he made two out of his most prominent works. Their initial wedded life was loaded up with happiness.

He started composing his show-stopper, War and Peace in 1862. The six volumes of the work were distributed somewhere in the range of 1863 and 1869. With 580 characters got from history and others made by Tolstoy, this extraordinary novel takes on investigating the hypothesis of history and the irrelevance of noted figures like Alexander and Napoleon. Anna Karenina, Tolstoy's next epic was begun in 1873 and distributed totally in 1878.

Contents

BOOK FIFTEEN : 1812 - 13

CHAPTER I

When seeing a dying animal a man feels a sense of horror: substance similar to his own is perishing before his eyes. But when it is a beloved and intimate human being that is dying, besides this horror at the extinction of life there is a severance, a spiritual wound, which like a physical wound is sometimes fatal and sometimes heals, but always aches and shrinks at any external irritating touch.

After Prince Andrew's death Natásha and Princess Mary alike felt this. Drooping in spirit and closing their eyes before the menacing cloud of death that overhung them, they dared not look life in the face. They carefully guarded their open wounds from any rough and painful contact. Everything: a carriage passing rapidly in the street, a summons to dinner, the maid's inquiry what dress to prepare, or worse still any word of insincere or feeble sympathy, seemed an insult, painfully irritated the wound, interrupting that necessary quiet in which they both tried to listen to the stern and dreadful choir that still resounded in their imagination, and hindered their gazing into those mysterious limitless vistas that for an instant had opened out before them.

Only when alone together were they free from such outrage and pain. They spoke little even to one another, and when they did it was of very unimportant matters.

Both avoided any allusion to the future. To admit the possibility of a future seemed to them to insult his memory. Still more carefully did they avoid anything relating to him who was dead. It seemed to them that what they had lived through and experienced could not be expressed in words, and that any reference to the details of his life infringed the majesty and sacredness of the mystery that had been accomplished before their eyes.

Continued abstention from speech, and constant avoidance of everything that might lead up to the subject—this halting on all sides at the boundary of what they might not mention—brought before their minds with still greater purity and clearness what they were both feeling.

But pure and complete sorrow is as impossible as pure and complete joy. Princess Mary, in her position as absolute and independent arbiter of her own fate and guardian and instructor of her nephew, was the first to be called back to life from that realm of sorrow in which she had dwelt for the first fortnight. She received letters from her relations to which she had to reply; the room in which little Nicholas had been put was damp and he began to cough; Alpátych came to Yaroslávl with reports on the state of their affairs and with advice and suggestions that they should return to Moscow to the house on the Vozdvízhenka Street, which had remained uninjured and needed only slight repairs. Life did not stand still and it was necessary to live. Hard as it was for Princess Mary to emerge from the realm of secluded contemplation in which she had lived till then, and sorry and almost ashamed as she felt to leave Natásha alone, yet the cares of life demanded her attention and she involuntarily yielded to them. She went through the accounts with Alpátych, conferred with Dessalles about her nephew, and gave orders and made preparations for the journey to Moscow.

Natásha remained alone and, from the time Princess Mary began making preparations for departure, held aloof from her too.

Princess Mary asked the countess to let Natásha go with her to Moscow, and both parents gladly accepted this offer, for they saw their daughter losing strength every day and thought that a change of scene and the advice of Moscow doctors would be good for her.

"I am not going anywhere," Natásha replied when this was proposed to her. "Do please just leave me alone!" And she ran out of the room, with difficulty refraining from tears of vexation and irritation rather than of sorrow.

After she felt herself deserted by Princes Mary and alone in her grief, Natásha spent most of the time in her room by herself, sitting huddled up feet and all in the corner of the sofa, tearing and twisting something with her slender nervous fingers and gazing intently and fixedly at whatever her eyes chanced to fall on. This solitude exhausted and tormented her but she was in absolute need of it. As soon as anyone entered she got up quickly, changed her position and expression, and picked up a book or some sewing, evidently waiting impatiently for the intruder to go.

She felt all the time as if she might at any moment penetrate that on which—with a terrible questioning too great for her strength—her spiritual gaze was fixed.

One day toward the end of December Natásha, pale and thin, dressed in a black woolen gown, her plaited hair negligently twisted into a knot, was crouched feet and all in the corner of her sofa, nervously crumpling and smoothing out the end of her sash while she looked at a corner of the door.

She was gazing in the direction in which he had gone—to the other side of life. And that other side of life, of which she had never before thought and which had formerly seemed to her so far away and improbable, was now nearer and more akin and more comprehensible than this side of life, where everything was either emptiness and desolation or suffering and indignity.

She was gazing where she knew him to be; but she could not imagine him otherwise than as he had been here. She now saw him again as he had been at Mytíshchi, at Tróitsa, and at Yaroslávl.

She saw his face, heard his voice, repeated his words and her own, and sometimes devised other words they might have spoken.

There he is lying back in an armchair in his velvet cloak, leaning his head on his thin pale hand. His chest is dreadfully hollow and his shoulders raised. His lips are firmly closed, his eyes glitter, and a wrinkle comes and goes on his pale forehead. One of his legs twitches just perceptibly, but rapidly. Natásha knows that he is struggling with terrible pain. "What is that pain like? Why does he have that pain? What does he feel? How does it hurt him?" thought Natásha. He noticed her watching him, raised his eyes, and began to speak seriously:

"One thing would be terrible," said he: "to bind oneself forever to a suffering man. It would be continual torture." And he looked searchingly at her. Natásha as usual answered before she had time to think what she would say. She said: "This can't go on—it won't. You will get well—quite well."

She now saw him from the commencement of that scene and relived what she had then felt. She recalled his long sad and severe look at those words and understood the meaning of the rebuke and despair in that protracted gaze.

"I agreed," Natásha now said to herself, "that it would be dreadful if he always continued to suffer. I said it then only because it would have been dreadful for him, but he understood it differently. He thought it would be dreadful for me. He then still wished to live and feared death. And I said it so awkwardly and stupidly! I did not say what I meant. I thought quite differently. Had I said what I thought, I should have said: even if he had to go on dying, to die continually before my eyes, I should have been happy compared with what I am now. Now there is nothing... nobody. Did he know that? No, he did not and never will know it. And now it will never, never be possible to put it right." And now he again seemed to be saying the same words to her, only in her imagination Natásha this time gave him a different answer. She stopped him and said: "Terrible for you, but not for me! You know that for me there is nothing in life but you, and to suffer with you is the greatest happiness for me," and he took her hand and pressed it as he had pressed it that terrible evening four days before his death. And in her imagination she said other tender and loving words which she might have said then but only spoke now: "I love thee!... thee! I love, love..." she said, convulsively pressing her hands and setting her teeth with a desperate effort....

She was overcome by sweet sorrow and tears were already rising in her eyes; then she suddenly asked herself to whom she was saying this. Again everything was shrouded in hard, dry perplexity, and again with a strained frown she peered toward the world where he was. And now, now it seemed to her she was penetrating the mystery.... But at the instant when it seemed that the incomprehensible was revealing itself to her a loud rattle of the door handle struck painfully on her ears. Dunyásha, her maid, entered the room quickly and abruptly with a frightened look on her face and showing no concern for her mistress.

"Come to your Papa at once, please!" said she with a strange, excited look. "A misfortune... about Peter Ilýnich... a letter," she finished with a sob.

CHAPTER II

Besides a feeling of aloofness from everybody Natásha was feeling a special estrangement from the members of her own family. All of them—her father, mother, and Sónya—were so near to her, so familiar, so commonplace, that all their words and feelings seemed an insult to the world in which she had been living of late, and she felt not merely indifferent to them but regarded them with hostility. She heard Dunyásha's words about Peter Ilýnich and a misfortune, but did not grasp them.

"What misfortune? What misfortune can happen to them? They just live their own old, quiet, and commonplace life," thought Natásha.

As she entered the ballroom her father was hurriedly coming out of her mother's room. His face was puckered up and wet with tears. He had evidently run out of that room to give vent to the sobs that were choking him. When he saw Natásha he waved his arms despairingly and burst into convulsively painful sobs that distorted his soft round face.

"Pe... Pétya... Go, go, she... is calling..." and weeping like a child and quickly shuffling on his feeble legs to a chair, he almost fell into it, covering his face with his hands.

Suddenly an electric shock seemed to run through Natásha's whole being. Terrible anguish struck her heart, she felt a dreadful ache as if something was being torn inside her and she were dying. But the pain was immediately followed by a feeling of release from the oppressive constraint that had prevented her taking part in life. The sight of her father, the terribly wild cries of her mother that she heard through the door, made her immediately forget herself and her own grief.

She ran to her father, but he feebly waved his arm, pointing to her mother's door. Princess Mary, pale and with quivering chin, came out from that room and taking Natásha by the arm said something to her. Natásha neither saw nor heard her. She went in with rapid steps, pausing at the door for an instant as if struggling with herself, and then ran to her mother.

The countess was lying in an armchair in a strange and awkward position, stretching out and beating her head against the wall. Sónya and the maids were holding her arms.

"Natásha! Natásha!..." cried the countess. "It's not true... it's not true... He's lying... Natásha!" she shrieked, pushing those around her away. "Go away, all of you; it's not true! Killed!... ha, ha, ha!... It's not true!"

Natásha put one knee on the armchair, stooped over her mother, embraced her, and with unexpected strength raised her, turned her face toward herself, and clung to her.

"Mummy!... darling!... I am here, my dearest Mummy," she kept on whispering, not pausing an instant.

She did not let go of her mother but struggled tenderly with her, demanded a pillow and hot water, and unfastened and tore open her mother's dress.

"My dearest darling.,. Mummy, my precious!..." she whispered incessantly, kissing her head, her hands, her face, and feeling her own irrepressible and streaming tears tickling her nose and cheeks.

The countess pressed her daughter's hand, closed her eyes, and became quiet for a moment. Suddenly she sat up with unaccustomed swiftness, glanced vacantly around her, and seeing Natásha began to press her daughter's head with all her strength. Then she turned toward her daughter's face which was wincing with pain and gazed long at it.

"Natásha, you love me?" she said in a soft trustful whisper. "Natásha, you would not deceive me? You'll tell me the whole truth?"

Natásha looked at her with eyes full of tears and in her look there was nothing but love and an entreaty for forgiveness.

"My darling Mummy!" she repeated, straining all the power of her love to find some way of taking on herself the excess of grief that crushed her mother.

And again in a futile struggle with reality her mother, refusing to believe that she could live when her beloved boy was killed in the bloom of life, escaped from reality into a world of delirium.

Natásha did not remember how that day passed nor that night, nor the next day and night. She did not sleep and did not leave her mother. Her persevering and patient love seemed completely to surround the countess every moment, not explaining or consoling, but recalling her to life.

During the third night the countess kept very quiet for a few minutes, and Natásha rested her head on the arm of her chair and closed her eyes, but opened them again on hearing the bedstead creak. The countess was sitting up in bed and speaking softly.

"How glad I am you have come. You are tired. Won't you have some tea?" Natásha went up to her. "You have improved in looks and grown more manly," continued the countess, taking her daughter's hand.

"Mamma! What are you saying..."

"Natásha, he is no more, no more!"

And embracing her daughter, the countess began to weep for the first time.

CHAPTER III

Princess Mary postponed her departure. Sónya and the count tried to replace Natásha but could not. They saw that she alone was able to restrain her mother from unreasoning despair. For three weeks Natásha remained constantly at her mother's side, sleeping on a lounge chair in her room, making her eat and drink, and talking to her incessantly because the mere sound of her tender, caressing tones soothed her mother.

The mother's wounded spirit could not heal. Pétya's death had torn from her half her life. When the news of Pétya's death had come she had been a fresh and vigorous woman of fifty, but a month later she left her room a listless old woman taking no interest in life. But the same blow that almost killed the countess, this second blow, restored Natásha to life.

A spiritual wound produced by a rending of the spiritual body is like a physical wound and, strange as it may seem, just as a deep wound may heal and its edges join, physical and spiritual wounds alike can yet heal completely only as the result of a vital force from within.

Natásha's wound healed in that way. She thought her life was ended, but her love for her mother unexpectedly showed her that the essence of life—love—was still active within her. Love awoke and so did life.

Prince Andrew's last days had bound Princess Mary and Natásha together; this new sorrow brought them still closer to one another. Princess Mary put off her departure, and for three weeks looked after

Natásha as if she had been a sick child. The last weeks passed in her mother's bedroom had strained Natásha's physical strength.

One afternoon noticing Natásha shivering with fever, Princess Mary took her to her own room and made her lie down on the bed. Natásha lay down, but when Princess Mary had drawn the blinds and was going away she called her back.

"I don't want to sleep, Mary, sit by me a little."

"You are tired—try to sleep."

"No, no. Why did you bring me away? She will be asking for me."

"She is much better. She spoke so well today," said Princess Mary.

Natásha lay on the bed and in the semidarkness of the room scanned Princess Mary's face.

"Is she like him?" thought Natásha. "Yes, like and yet not like. But she is quite original, strange, new, and unknown. And she loves me. What is in her heart? All that is good. But how? What is her mind like? What does she think about me? Yes, she is splendid!"

"Mary," she said timidly, drawing Princess Mary's hand to herself, "Mary, you mustn't think me wicked. No? Mary darling, how I love you! Let us be quite, quite friends."

And Natásha, embracing her, began kissing her face and hands, making Princess Mary feel shy but happy by this demonstration of her feelings.

From that day a tender and passionate friendship such as exists only between women was established between Princess Mary and Natásha. They were continually kissing and saying tender things to one another and spent most of their time together. When one went out the other became restless and hastened to rejoin her. Together they felt more in harmony with one another than either of them felt with herself when alone. A feeling stronger than friendship sprang up between them; an exclusive feeling of life being possible only in each other's presence.

Sometimes they were silent for hours; sometimes after they were already in bed they would begin talking and go on till morning. They spoke most of what was long past. Princess Mary spoke of her childhood, of her mother, her father, and her daydreams; and Natásha, who with a passive lack of understanding had formerly turned away from that life of devotion, submission, and the poetry of Christian self-sacrifice, now feeling herself bound to Princess Mary by affection, learned to love her past too and to understand a side of life previously incomprehensible to her. She did not think of applying submission and self-abnegation to her own life, for she was accustomed to seek other joys, but she understood and loved in another those previously incomprehensible virtues. For Princess Mary, listening to Natásha's tales of childhood and early youth, there also opened out a new and hitherto uncomprehended side of life: belief in life and its enjoyment.

Just as before, they never mentioned *him* so as not to lower (as they thought) their exalted feelings by words; but this silence about him had the effect of making them gradually begin to forget him without being conscious of it.

Natásha had grown thin and pale and physically so weak that they all talked about her health, and this pleased her. But sometimes she was suddenly overcome by fear not only of death but of sickness, weakness, and loss of good looks, and involuntarily she examined her bare arm carefully, surprised at its thinness, and in the morning noticed her drawn and, as it seemed to her, piteous face in her glass. It seemed to her that things must be so, and yet it was dreadfully sad.

One day she went quickly upstairs and found herself out of breath. Unconsciously she immediately invented a reason for going down, and then, testing her strength, ran upstairs again, observing the result.

Another time when she called Dunyásha her voice trembled, so she called again—though she could hear Dunyásha coming—called her in the deep chest tones in which she had been wont to sing, and listened attentively to herself.

She did not know and would not have believed it, but beneath the layer of slime that covered her soul and seemed to her impenetrable, delicate young shoots of grass were already sprouting, which taking root would so cover with their living verdure the grief that weighed her down that it would soon no longer be seen or noticed. The wound had begun to heal from within.

At the end of January Princess Mary left for Moscow, and the count insisted on Natásha's going with her to consult the doctors.

CHAPTER IV

After the encounter at Vyázma, where Kutúzov had been unable to hold back his troops in their anxiety to overwhelm and cut off the enemy and so on, the farther movement of the fleeing French, and of the Russians who pursued them, continued as far as Krásnoe without a battle. The flight was so rapid that the Russian army pursuing the French could not keep up with them; cavalry and artillery horses broke down, and the information received of the movements of the French was never reliable.

The men in the Russian army were so worn out by this continuous marching at the rate of twenty-seven miles a day that they could not go any faster.

To realize the degree of exhaustion of the Russian army it is only necessary to grasp clearly the meaning of the fact that, while not losing more than five thousand killed and wounded after Tarútino and less than a hundred prisoners, the Russian army which left that place a hundred thousand strong reached Krásnoe with only fifty thousand.

The rapidity of the Russian pursuit was just as destructive to our army as the flight of the French was to theirs. The only difference was that the Russian army moved voluntarily, with no such threat of destruction as hung over the French, and that the sick Frenchmen were left behind in enemy hands while the sick Russians left behind were among their own people. The chief cause of the wastage of Napoleon's army was the rapidity of its movement, and a convincing proof of this is the corresponding decrease of the Russian army.

Kutúzov as far as was in his power, instead of trying to check the movement of the French as was desired in Petersburg and by the Russian army generals, directed his whole activity here, as he had done at Tarútino and Vyázma, to hastening it on while easing the movement of our army.

But besides this, since the exhaustion and enormous diminution of the army caused by the rapidity of the advance had become evident, another reason for slackening the pace and delaying presented itself to Kutúzov. The aim of the Russian army was to pursue the French. The road the French would take was unknown, and so the closer our troops trod on their heels the greater distance they had to cover. Only by following at some distance could one cut across the zigzag path of the French. All the artful maneuvers suggested by our generals meant fresh movements of the army and a lengthening of its marches, whereas the only reasonable aim was to shorten those marches. To that end Kutúzov's activity was directed during the whole campaign from Moscow to Vílna—not casually or intermittently but so consistently that he never once deviated from it.

Kutúzov felt and knew—not by reasoning or science but with the whole of his Russian being—what every Russian soldier felt: that the French were beaten, that the enemy was flying and must be driven out; but at the same time he like the soldiers realized all the hardship of this march, the rapidity of which was unparalleled for such a time of the year.

But to the generals, especially the foreign ones in the Russian army, who wished to distinguish themselves, to astonish somebody, and for some reason to capture a king or a duke—it seemed that now—when any battle must be horrible and senseless—was the very time to fight and conquer somebody. Kutúzov merely shrugged his shoulders when one after another they presented projects of maneuvers to be made with those soldiers—ill-shod, insufficiently clad, and half starved—who within a month and without fighting a battle had dwindled to half their number, and who at the best if the flight continued would have to go a greater distance than they had already traversed, before they reached the frontier.

This longing to distinguish themselves, to maneuver, to overthrow, and to cut off showed itself particularly whenever the Russians stumbled on the French army.

So it was at Krásnoe, where they expected to find one of the three French columns and stumbled instead on Napoleon himself with sixteen thousand men. Despite all Kutúzov's efforts to avoid that ruinous encounter and to preserve his troops, the massacre of the broken mob of French soldiers by worn-out Russians continued at Krásnoe for three days.

Toll wrote a disposition: "The first column will march to so and so," etc. And as usual nothing happened in accord with the disposition. Prince Eugène of Württemberg fired from a hill over the French crowds that were running past, and demanded reinforcements which did not arrive. The French, avoiding the Russians, dispersed and hid themselves in the forest by night, making their way round as best they could, and continued their flight.

Milorádovich, who said he did not want to know anything about the commissariat affairs of his detachment, and could never be found when he was wanted—that *chevalier sans peuret sans reproche* * as he styled himself—who was fond of parleys with the French, sent envoys demanding their surrender, wasted time, and did not do what he was ordered to do.

* Knight without fear and without reproach.

"I give you that column, lads," he said, riding up to the troops and pointing out the French to the cavalry.

And the cavalry, with spurs and sabers urging on horses that could scarcely move, trotted with much effort to the column presented to them—that is to say, to a crowd of Frenchmen stark with cold, frost-bitten, and starving—and the column that had been presented to them threw down its arms and surrendered as it had long been anxious to do.

At Krásnoe they took twenty-six thousand prisoners, several hundred cannon, and a stick called a "marshal's staff," and disputed as to who had distinguished himself and were pleased with their achievement—though they much regretted not having taken Napoleon, or at least a marshal or a hero of some sort, and reproached one another and especially Kutúzov for having failed to do so.

These men, carried away by their passions, were but blind tools of the most melancholylaw of necessity, but considered themselves heroes and imagined that they were accomplishing a most noble and honorable deed. They blamed Kutúzov and said that from the very beginning of the campaign he had prevented their vanquishing Napoleon, that he thought of nothing but satisfying his passions and would not advance from the Linen Factories because he was comfortable there, that at Krásnoe he checked the advance because on learning that Napoleon was there he had quite lost his head, and that it was probable that he had an understanding with Napoleon and had been bribed by him, and so on, and so on.

Not only did his contemporaries, carried away by their passions, talk in this way, but posterity and history have acclaimed Napoleon as *grand*, while Kutúzov is described by foreigners as a crafty, dissolute, weak old courtier, and by Russians as something indefinite—a sort of puppet useful only because he had a Russian name.

CHAPTER V

In 1812 and 1813 Kutúzov was openly accused of blundering. The Emperor was dissatisfied with him. And in a history recently written by order of the Highest Authorities it is said that Kutúzov was a cunning court liar, frightened of the name of Napoleon, and that by his blunders at Krásnoe and the Berëzina he deprived the Russian army of the glory of complete victory over the French. *

* *History of the year 1812. The character of Kutúzov and reflections on the unsatisfactory results of the battles at Krásnoe*, by Bogdánovich.

Such is the fate not of great men (*grands hommes*) whom the Russian mind does not acknowledge, but of those rare and always solitary individuals who, discerning the will of Providence, submit their personal will to it. The hatred and contempt of the crowd punish such men for discerning the higher laws.

For Russian historians, strange and terrible to say, Napoleon—that most insignificant tool of history who never anywhere, even in exile, showed human dignity—Napoleon is the object of adulation and enthusiasm; he is *grand*. But Kutúzov—the man who from the beginning to the end of his activity in 1812, never once swerving by word or deed from Borodinó to Vílna, presented an example exceptional in history of self-sacrifice and a present consciousness of the future importance of what was happening—Kutúzov seems to them something indefinite and pitiful, and when speaking of him and of the year 1812 they always seem a little ashamed.

And yet it is difficult to imagine an historical character whose activity was so unswervingly directed to a single aim; and it would be difficult to imagine any aim more worthy or more consonant with the will of the whole people. Still more difficult would it be to find an instance in history of the aim of an historical personage being so completely accomplished as that to which all Kutúzov's efforts were directed in 1812.

Kutúzov never talked of "forty centuries looking down from the Pyramids," of the sacrifices he offered for the fatherland, or of what he intended to accomplish or had accomplished; in general he said nothing about himself, adopted no pose, always appeared to be the simplest and most ordinary of men, and said the simplest and most ordinary things. He wrote letters to his daughters and to Madame de Staël, read novels, liked the society of pretty women, jested with generals, officers, and soldiers, and never contradicted those who tried to prove anything to him. When Count Rostopchín at the Yaúza bridge galloped up to Kutúzov with personal reproaches for having caused the destruction of Moscow, and said: "How was it you promised not to abandon Moscow without a battle?" Kutúzov replied: "And I shall not abandon Moscow without a battle," though Moscow was then already abandoned. When Arakchéev, coming to him from the Emperor, said that Ermólov ought to be appointed chief of the artillery, Kutúzov replied: "Yes, I was just saying so myself," though a moment before he had said quite the contrary. What did it matter to him—who then alone amid a senseless crowd understood the whole tremendous significance of what was happening—what did it matter to him whether Rostopchín attributed the calamities of Moscow to him or to himself? Still less could it matter to him who was appointed chief of the artillery.

Not merely in these cases but continually did that old man—who by experience of life had reached the conviction that thoughts and the words serving as their expression are not what move people—use quite meaningless words that happened to enter his head.

But that man, so heedless of his words, did not once during the whole time of his activity utter one word inconsistent with the single aim toward which he moved throughout the whole war. Obviously in spite of himself, in very diverse circumstances, he repeatedly expressed his real thoughts with the bitter conviction that he would not be understood. Beginning with the battle of Borodinó, from which time his disagreement with those about him began, he alone said that *the battle of Borodinó was a victory*, and repeated this both verbally and in his dispatches and reports up to the time of his death.

He alone said that *the loss of Moscow is not the loss of Russia*. In reply to Lauriston's proposal of peace, he said: *There can be no peace, for such is the people's will.* He alone during the retreat of the French said that *all our maneuvers are useless, everything is being accomplished of itself better than we could desire; that the enemy must be offered "a golden bridge"*; that *neither the Tarútino, the Vyázma, nor the Krásnoe battles were necessary*; that *we must keep some force to reach the frontier with,* and that *he would not sacrifice a single Russian for ten Frenchmen.*

And this courtier, as he is described to us, who lies to Arakchéev to please the Emperor, he alone—incurring thereby the Emperor's displeasure—said in Vílna that *to carry the war beyond the frontier is useless and harmful.*

Nor do words alone prove that only he understood the meaning of the events. His actions—without the smallest deviation—were all directed to one and the same threefold end: (1) to brace all his strength for conflict with the French, (2) to defeat them, and (3) to drive them out of Russia, minimizing as far as possible the sufferings of our people and of our army.

This procrastinator Kutúzov, whose motto was "Patience and Time," this enemy of decisive action, gave battle at Borodinó, investing the preparations for it with unparalleled solemnity. This Kutúzov who before the battle of Austerlitz began said that it would be lost, he alone, in contradiction to everyone else, declared till his death that Borodinó was a victory, despite the assurance of generals that the battle was lost and despite the fact that for an army to have to retire after winning a battle was unprecedented. He alone during the whole retreat insisted that battles, which were useless then, should not be fought, and that a new war should not be begun nor the frontiers of Russia crossed.

It is easy now to understand the significance of these events—if only we abstain from attributing to the activity of the mass aims that existed only in the heads of a dozen individuals—for the events and results now lie before us.

But how did that old man, alone, in opposition to the general opinion, so truly discern the importance of the people's view of the events that in all his activity he was never once untrue to it?

The source of that extraordinary power of penetrating the meaning of the events then occuring lay in the national feeling which he possessed in full purity and strength.

Only the recognition of the fact that he possessed this feeling caused the people in so strange a manner, contrary to the Tsar's wish, to select him—an old man in disfavor—to be their representative in the national war. And only that feeling placed him on that highest human pedestal from which he, the commander in chief, devoted all his powers not to slaying and destroying men but to saving and showing pity on them.

That simple, modest, and therefore truly great, figure could not be cast in the false moldof a European hero—the supposed ruler of men—that history has invented.

To a lackey no man can be great, for a lackey has his own conception of greatness.

CHAPTER VI

The fifth of November was the first day of what is called the battle of Krásnoe. Toward evening—after much disputing and many mistakes made by generals who did not go to their proper places, and after adjutants had been sent about with counterorders—when it had become plain that the enemy was everywhere in flight and that there could and would be no battle, Kutúzov left Krásnoe and went to Dóbroe whither his headquarters had that day been transferred.

The day was clear and frosty. Kutúzov rode to Dóbroe on his plump little white horse, followed by an enormous suite of discontented generals who whispered among themselves behind his back. All along the road groups of French prisoners captured that day (there were seven thousand of them) were crowding to warm themselves at campfires. Near Dóbroe an immense crowd of tattered prisoners, buzzing with talk and wrapped and bandaged in anything they had been able to get hold of, were standing in the road beside a long row of unharnessed French guns. At the approach of the commander in chief the buzz of talk ceased and all eyes were fixed on Kutúzov who, wearing a white cap with a red band and a padded overcoat that bulged on his round shoulders, moved slowly along the road on his white horse. One of the generals was reporting to him where the guns and prisoners had been captured.

Kutúzov seemed preoccupied and did not listen to what the general was saying. He screwed up his eyes with a dissatisfied look as he gazed attentively and fixedly at these prisoners, who presented a specially wretched appearance. Most of them were disfigured by frost-bitten noses and cheeks, and nearly all had red, swollen and festering eyes.

One group of the French stood close to the road, and two of them, one of whom had his face covered with sores, were tearing a piece of raw flesh with their hands. There was something horrible and bestial in the fleeting glance they threw at the riders and in the malevolent expression with which, after a glance at Kutúzov, the soldier with the sores immediately turned away and went on with what he was doing.

Kutúzov looked long and intently at these two soldiers. He puckered his face, screwed up his eyes, and pensively swayed his head. At another spot he noticed a Russian soldier laughingly patting a Frenchman on the shoulder, saying something to him in a friendly manner, and Kutúzov with the same expression on his face again swayed his head.

"What were you saying?" he asked the general, who continuing his report directed the commander in chief's attention to some standards captured from the French and standing in front of the Preobrazhénsk regiment.

"Ah, the standards!" said Kutúzov, evidently detaching himself with difficulty from the thoughts that preoccupied him.

He looked about him absently. Thousands of eyes were looking at him from all sides awaiting a word from him.

He stopped in front of the Preobrazhénsk regiment, sighed deeply, and closed his eyes. One of his suite beckoned to the soldiers carrying the standards to advance and surround the commander in chief with them. Kutúzov was silent for a few seconds and then, submitting with evident reluctance to the duty imposed by his position, raised his head and began to speak. A throng of officers surrounded him. He looked attentively around at the circle of officers, recognizing several of them.

"I thank you all!" he said, addressing the soldiers and then again the officers. In the stillness around him his slowly uttered words were distinctly heard. "I thank you all for your hard and faithful service. The victory is complete and Russia will not forget you! Honor to you forever."

He paused and looked around.

"Lower its head, lower it!" he said to a soldier who had accidentally lowered the French eagle he was holding before the Preobrazhénsk standards. "Lower, lower, that's it. Hurrah lads!" he added, addressing the men with a rapid movement of his chin.

"Hur-r-rah!" roared thousands of voices.

While the soldiers were shouting Kutúzov leaned forward in his saddle and bowed his head, and his eye lit up with a mild and apparently ironic gleam.

"You see, brothers..." said he when the shouts had ceased... and all at once his voice and the expression of his face changed. It was no longer the commander in chief speaking but an ordinary old man who wanted to tell his comrades something very important.

There was a stir among the throng of officers and in the ranks of the soldiers, who moved that they might hear better what he was going to say.

"You see, brothers, I know it's hard for you, but it can't be helped! Bear up; it won't be for long now! We'll see our visitors off and then we'll rest. The Tsar won't forget your service. It is hard for you, but still you are at home while they—you see what they have come to," said he, pointing to the prisoners. "Worse off than our poorest beggars. While they were strong we didn't spare ourselves, but now we may even pity them. They are human beings too. Isn't it so, lads?"

He looked around, and in the direct, respectful, wondering gaze fixed upon him he read sympathy with what he had said. His face grew brighter and brighter with an old man's mild smile, which drew the corners of his lips and eyes into a cluster of wrinkles. He ceased speaking and bowed his head as if in perplexity.

"But after all who asked them here? Serves them right, the bloody bastards!" he cried, suddenly lifting his head.

And flourishing his whip he rode off at a gallop for the first time during the whole campaign, and left the broken ranks of the soldiers laughing joyfully and shouting "Hurrah!"

Kutúzov's words were hardly understood by the troops. No one could have repeated the field marshal's address, begun solemnly and then changing into an old man's simplehearted talk; but the hearty sincerity of that speech, the feeling of majestic triumph combined with pity for the foe and consciousness of the justice of our cause, exactly expressed by that old man's good-natured expletives, was not merely understood but lay in the soul of every soldier and found expression in their joyous and long-sustained shouts. Afterwards when one of the generals addressed Kutúzov asking whether he wished his *calèche* to be sent for, Kutúzov in answering unexpectedly gave a sob, being evidently greatly moved.

CHAPTER VII

When the troops reached their night's halting place on the eighth of November, the last day of the Krásnoe battles, it was already growing dusk. All day it had been calm and frosty with occasional lightly falling snow and toward evening it began to clear. Through the falling snow a purple-black and starry sky showed itself and the frost grew keener.

An infantry regiment which had left Tarútino three thousand strong but now numbered only nine hundred was one of the first to arrive that night at its halting place—a village on the highroad. The quartermasters who met the regiment announced that all the huts were full of sick and dead Frenchmen, cavalrymen, and members of the staff. There was only one hut available for the regimental commander.

The commander rode up to his hut. The regiment passed through the village and stacked its arms in front of the last huts.

Like some huge many-limbed animal, the regiment began to prepare its lair and its food. One part of it dispersed and waded knee-deep through the snow into a birch forest to the right of the village, and immediately the sound of axes and swords, the crashing of branches, and merry voices could be heard from there. Another section amid the regimental wagons and horses which were standing in a group was busy getting out caldrons and rye biscuit, and feeding the horses. A third section scattered through the village arranging quarters for the staff officers, carrying out the French corpses that were in the huts, and dragging away boards, dry wood, and thatch from the roofs, for the campfires, or wattle fences to serve for shelter.

Some fifteen men with merry shouts were shaking down the high wattle wall of a shed, the roof of which had already been removed.

"Now then, all together—shove!" cried the voices, and the huge surface of the wall, sprinkled with snow and creaking with frost, was seen swaying in the gloom of the night. The lower stakes cracked more and more and at last the wall fell, and with it the men who had been pushing it. Loud, coarse laughter and joyous shouts ensued.

"Now then, catch hold in twos! Hand up the lever! That's it.... Where are you shoving to?"

"Now, all together! But wait a moment, boys... With a song!"

All stood silent, and a soft, pleasant velvety voice began to sing. At the end of the third verse as the last note died away, twenty voices roared out at once: "Oo-oo-oo-oo! That's it. All together! Heave away, boys!..." but despite their united efforts the wattle hardly moved, and in the silence that followed the heavy breathing of the men was audible.

"Here, you of the Sixth Company! Devils that you are! Lend a hand... will you? You may want us one of these days."

Some twenty men of the Sixth Company who were on their way into the village joined the haulers, and the wattle wall, which was about thirty-five feet long and seven feet high, moved forward along the village street, swaying, pressing upon and cutting the shoulders of the gasping men.

"Get along... Falling? What are you stopping for? There now...."

Merry senseless words of abuse flowed freely.

"What are you up to?" suddenly came the authoritative voice of a sergeant major who came upon the men who were hauling their burden. "There are gentry here; the general himself is in that hut, and you foul-mouthed devils, you brutes, I'll give it to you!" shouted he, hitting the first man who came in his way a swinging blow on the back. "Can't you make less noise?"

The men became silent. The soldier who had been struck groaned and wiped his face, which had been scratched till it bled by his falling against the wattle.

"There, how that devil hits out! He's made my face all bloody," said he in a frightened whisper when the sergeant major had passed on.

"Don't you like it?" said a laughing voice, and moderating their tones the men moved forward.

When they were out of the village they began talking again as loud as before, interlarding their talk with the same aimless expletives.

In the hut which the men had passed, the chief officers had gathered and were in animated talk over their tea about the events of the day and the maneuvers suggested for tomorrow. It was proposed to make a flank march to the left, cut off the Vice-King (Murat) and capture him.

By the time the soldiers had dragged the wattle fence to its place the campfires were blazing on all sides ready for cooking, the wood crackled, the snow was melting, and black shadows of soldiers flitted to and fro all over the occupied space where the snow had been trodden down.

Axes and choppers were plied all around. Everything was done without any orders being given. Stores of wood were brought for the night, shelters were rigged up for the officers, caldrons were being boiled, and muskets and accouterments put in order.

The wattle wall the men had brought was set up in a semicircle by the Eighth Company as a shelter from the north, propped up by musket rests, and a campfire was built before it. They beat the tattoo, called the roll, had supper, and settled down round the fires for the night—some repairing their footgear, some smoking pipes, and some stripping themselves naked to steam the lice out of their shirts.

CHAPTER VIII

One would have thought that under the almost incredibly wretched conditions the Russian soldiers were in at that time—lacking warm boots and sheepskin coats, without a roof over their heads, in the snow with eighteen degrees of frost, and without even full rations (the commissariat did not always keep up with the troops)—they would have presented a very sad and depressing spectacle.

On the contrary, the army had never under the best material conditions presented a more cheerful and animated aspect. This was because all who began to grow depressed or who lost strength were sifted out of the army day by day. All the physically or morally weak had long since been left behind and only the flower of the army—physically and mentally—remained.

More men collected behind the wattle fence of the Eighth Company than anywhere else. Two sergeants major were sitting with them and their campfire blazed brighter than others. For leave to sit by their wattle they demanded contributions of fuel.

"Eh, Makéev! What has become of you, you son of a bitch? Are you lost or have the wolves eaten you? Fetch some more wood!" shouted a red-haired and red-faced man, screwing up his eyes and blinking because of the smoke but not moving back from the fire. "And you, Jackdaw, go and fetch some wood!" said he to another soldier.

This red-haired man was neither a sergeant nor a corporal, but being robust he ordered about those weaker than himself. The soldier they called "Jackdaw," a thin little fellow with a sharp nose, rose obediently and was about to go but at that instant there came into the light of the fire the slender, handsome figure of a young soldier carrying a load of wood.

"Bring it here—that's fine!"

They split up the wood, pressed it down on the fire, blew at it with their mouths, and fanned it with the skirts of their greatcoats, making the flames hiss and crackle. The men drew nearer and lit their pipes. The handsome young soldier who had brought the wood, setting his arms akimbo, began stamping his cold feet rapidly and deftly on the spot where he stood.

"Mother! The dew is cold but clear.... It's well that I'm a musketeer..." he sang, pretending to hiccough after each syllable.

"Look out, your soles will fly off!" shouted the red-haired man, noticing that the sole of the dancer's boot was hanging loose. "What a fellow you are for dancing!"

The dancer stopped, pulled off the loose piece of leather, and threw it on the fire.

"Right enough, friend," said he, and, having sat down, took out of his knapsack a scrap of blue French cloth, and wrapped it round his foot. "It's the steam that spoils them," he added, stretching out his feet toward the fire.

"They'll soon be issuing us new ones. They say that when we've finished hammering *them*, we're to receive double kits!"

"And that son of a bitch Petróv has lagged behind after all, it seems," said one sergeant major.

"I've had an eye on him this long while," said the other.

"Well, he's a poor sort of soldier...."

"But in the Third Company they say nine men were missing yesterday."

"Yes, it's all very well, but when a man's feet are frozen how can he walk?"

"Eh? Don't talk nonsense!" said a sergeant major.

"Do you want to be doing the same?" said an old soldier, turning reproachfully to the man who had spoken of frozen feet.

"Well, you know," said the sharp-nosed man they called Jackdaw in a squeaky and unsteady voice, raising himself at the other side of the fire, "a plump man gets thin, but for a thin one it's death. Take me, now! I've got no strength left," he added, with sudden resolution turning to the sergeant major. "Tell them to send me to hospital; I'm aching all over; anyway I shan't be able to keep up."

"That'll do, that'll do!" replied the sergeant major quietly.

The soldier said no more and the talk went on.

"What a lot of those Frenchies were taken today, and the fact is that not one of them had what you might call real boots on," said a soldier, starting a new theme. "They were no more than make-believes."

"The Cossacks have taken their boots. They were clearing the hut for the colonel and carried them out. It was pitiful to see them, boys," put in the dancer. "As they turned them over one seemed still alive and, would you believe it, he jabbered something in their lingo."

"But they're a clean folk, lads," the first man went on; "he was white—as white as birchbark—and some of them are such fine fellows, you might think they were nobles."

"Well, what do you think? They make soldiers of all classes there."

"But they don't understand our talk at all," said the dancer with a puzzled smile. "I asked him whose subject he was, and he jabbered in his own way. A queer lot!"

"But it's strange, friends," continued the man who had wondered at their whiteness, "the peasants at Mozháysk were saying that when they began burying the dead—where the battle was you know—well, those dead had been lying there for nearly a month, and says the peasant, 'they lie as white as paper, clean, and not as much smell as a puff of powder smoke.'"

"Was it from the cold?" asked someone.

"You're a clever fellow! From the cold indeed! Why, it was hot. If it had been from the cold, ours would not have rotted either. 'But,' he says, 'go up to ours and they are all rotten and maggoty. So,' he says, 'we tie our faces up with kerchiefs and turn our heads away as we drag them off: we can hardly do it. But theirs,' he says, 'are white as paper and not so much smell as a whiff of gunpowder.'"

All were silent.

"It must be from their food," said the sergeant major. "They used to gobble the same food as the gentry."

No one contradicted him.

"That peasant near Mozháysk where the battle was said the men were all called up from ten villages around and they carted for twenty days and still didn't finish carting the dead away. And as for the wolves, he says..."

"That was a real battle," said an old soldier. "It's the only one worth remembering; but since that... it's only been tormenting folk."

"And do you know, Daddy, the day before yesterday we ran at them and, my word, they didn't let us get near before they just threw down their muskets and went on their knees. 'Pardon!' they say. That's only one case. They say Plátov took 'Poleon himself twice. But he didn't know the right charm. He catches him and catches him—no good! He turns into a bird in his hands and flies away. And there's no way of killing him either."

"You're a first-class liar, Kiselëv, when I come to look at you!"

"Liar, indeed! It's the real truth."

"If he fell into my hands, when I'd caught him I'd bury him in the ground with an aspen stake to fix him down. What a lot of men he's ruined!"

"Well, anyhow we're going to end it. He won't come here again," remarked the old soldier, yawning.

The conversation flagged, and the soldiers began settling down to sleep.

"Look at the stars. It's wonderful how they shine! You would think the women had spread out their linen," said one of the men, gazing with admiration at the Milky Way.

"That's a sign of a good harvest next year."

"We shall want some more wood."

"You warm your back and your belly gets frozen. That's queer."

"O Lord!"

"What are you pushing for? Is the fire only for you? Look how he's sprawling!"

In the silence that ensued, the snoring of those who had fallen asleep could be heard. Others turned over and warmed themselves, now and again exchanging a few words. From a campfire a hundred paces off came a sound of general, merry laughter.

"Hark at them roaring there in the Fifth Company!" said one of the soldiers, "and what a lot of them there are!"

One of the men got up and went over to the Fifth Company.

"They're having such fun," said he, coming back. "Two Frenchies have turned up. One's quite frozen and the other's an awful swaggerer. He's singing songs...."

"Oh, I'll go across and have a look...."

And several of the men went over to the Fifth Company.

CHAPTER IX

The Fifth company was bivouacking at the very edge of the forest. A huge campfire was blazing brightly in the midst of the snow, lighting up the branches of trees heavy with hoarfrost.

About midnight they heard the sound of steps in the snow of the forest, and the crackling of dry branches.

"A bear, lads," said one of the men.

They all raised their heads to listen, and out of the forest into the bright firelight stepped two strangely clad human figures clinging to one another.

These were two Frenchmen who had been hiding in the forest. They came up to the fire, hoarsely uttering something in a language our soldiers did not understand. One was taller than the other; he wore an officer's hat and seemed quite exhausted. On approaching the fire he had been going to sit down, but fell. The other, a short sturdy soldier with a shawl tied round his head, was stronger. He raised his companion and said something, pointing to his mouth. The soldiers surrounded the Frenchmen, spread a greatcoat on the ground for the sick man, and brought some buckwheat porridge and vodka for both of them.

The exhausted French officer was Ramballe and the man with his head wrapped in the shawl was Morel, his orderly.

When Morel had drunk some vodka and finished his bowl of porridge he suddenly became unnaturally merry and chattered incessantly to the soldiers, who could not understand him. Ramballe refused food and resting his head on his elbow lay silent beside the campfire, looking at the Russian soldiers with red and vacant eyes. Occasionally he emitted a long-drawn groan and then again became silent. Morel, pointing to his shoulders, tried to impress on the soldiers the fact that Ramballe was an officer and ought to be warmed. A Russian officer who had come up to the fire sent to ask his colonel whether he would not take a French officer into his hut to warm him, and when the messenger returned and said that the colonel wished the officer to be brought to him, Ramballe was told to go. He rose and tried to walk, but staggered and would have fallen had not a soldier standing by held him up.

"You won't do it again, eh?" said one of the soldiers, winking and turning mockingly to Ramballe.

"Oh, you fool! Why talk rubbish, lout that you are—a real peasant!" came rebukes from all sides addressed to the jesting soldier.

They surrounded Ramballe, lifted him on the crossed arms of two soldiers, and carried him to the hut. Ramballe put his arms around their necks while they carried him and began wailing plaintively:

"Oh, you fine fellows, my kind, kind friends! These are men! Oh, my brave, kind friends," and he leaned his head against the shoulder of one of the men like a child.

Meanwhile Morel was sitting in the best place by the fire, surrounded by the soldiers.

Morel, a short sturdy Frenchman with inflamed and streaming eyes, was wearing a woman's cloak and had a shawl tied woman fashion round his head over his cap. He was evidently tipsy, and was singing a French song in a hoarse broken voice, with an arm thrown round the nearest soldier. The soldiers simply held their sides as they watched him.

"Now then, now then, teach us how it goes! I'll soon pick it up. How is it?" said the man—a singer and a wag—whom Morel was embracing.

"Vive Henri Quatre! Viveceroi valiant!" sang Morel, winking. *"Ce diable à quatre..."* *

* "Long live Henry the Fourth, that valiant king! That rowdy devil."

"Vivarika! Vif-seruvaru! Sedyablyaka!" repeated the soldier, flourishing his arm and really catching the tune.

"Bravo! Ha, ha, ha!" rose their rough, joyous laughter from all sides.

Morel, wrinkling up his face, laughed too.

"Well, go on, go on!"

"Qui eut le triple talent, De boire, de battre, Et d'être un vert galant." *

* Who had a triple talent For drinking, for fighting, And for being a gallant old boy...

"It goes smoothly, too. Well, now, Zaletáev!"

"Ke..." Zaletáev, brought out with effort: "ke-e-e-e," he drawled, laboriously pursing his lips, "le-trip-ta-la-de-bu-de-ba, e de-tra-va-ga-la" he sang.

"Fine! Just like the Frenchie! Oh, hoho! Do you want some more to eat?"

"Give him some porridge: it takes a long time to get filled up after starving."

They gave him some more porridge and Morel with a laugh set to work on his third bowl. All the young soldiers smiled gaily as they watched him. The older men, who thought it undignified to amuse themselves with such nonsense, continued to lie at the opposite side of the fire, but one would occasionally raise himself on an elbow and glance at Morel with a smile.

"They are men too," said one of them as he wrapped himself up in his coat. "Even wormwood grows on its own root."

"O Lord, O Lord! How starry it is! Tremendous! That means a hard frost...."

They all grew silent. The stars, as if knowing that no one was looking at them, began to disport themselves in the dark sky: now flaring up, now vanishing, now trembling, they were busy whispering something gladsome and mysterious to one another.

CHAPTER X

The French army melted away at the uniform rate of a mathematical progression; and that crossing of the Berëzina about which so much has been written was only one intermediate stage in its destruction, and not at all the decisive episode of the campaign. If so much has been and still is written about the Berëzina, on the French side this is only because at the broken bridge across that river the calamities their army had been previously enduring were suddenly concentrated at one moment into a tragic spectacle that remained in every memory, and on the Russian side merely because in Petersburg—far from the seat of war—a plan (again one of Pfuel's) had been devised to catch Napoleon in a strategic trap at the Berëzina River. Everyone assured himself that all would happen according to plan, and therefore insisted that it was just the crossing of the Berëzina that destroyed the French army. In reality the results of the crossing were much less disastrous to the French—in guns and men lost—than Krásnoe had been, as the figures show.

The sole importance of the crossing of the Berëzina lies in the fact that it plainly and indubitably proved the fallacy of all the plans for cutting off the enemy's retreat and the soundness of the only possible line of action—the one Kutúzov and the general mass of the army demanded—namely, simply to follow the enemy up. The French crowd fled at a continually increasing speed and all its energy was directed to reaching its goal. It fled like a wounded animal and it was impossible to block its path. This was shown not so much by the arrangements it made for crossing as by what took place at the bridges. When the bridges broke down, unarmed soldiers, people from Moscow and women with children who were with the French transport, all—carried on by *vis inertiæ*—pressed forward into boats and into the ice-covered water and did not surrender.

That impulse was reasonable. The condition of fugitives and of pursuers was equally bad. As long as they remained with their own people each might hope for help from his fellows and the definite place he held among them. But those who surrendered, while remaining in the same pitiful plight, would be on a lower level to claim a share in the necessities of life. The French did not need to be informed of the fact that half the prisoners—with whom the Russians did not know what to do—perished of cold and hunger despite their captors' desire to save them; they felt that it could not be otherwise. The most compassionate Russian commanders, those favorable to the French—and even the Frenchmen in the Russian service—could do nothing for the prisoners. The French perished from the conditions to which the Russian army was itself exposed. It was impossible to take bread and clothes from our hungry and indispensable soldiers to give to the French who, though not harmful, or hated, or guilty, were simply unnecessary. Some Russians even did that, but they were exceptions.

Certain destruction lay behind the French but in front there was hope. Their ships had been burned, there was no salvation save in collective flight, and on that the whole strength of the French was concentrated.

The farther they fled the more wretched became the plight of the remnant, especially after the Berëzina, on which (in consequence of the Petersburg plan) special hopes had been placed by the Russians, and the keener grew the passions of the Russian commanders, who blamed one another and Kutúzov most of all. Anticipation that the failure of the Petersburg Berëzina plan would be attributed to Kutúzov led to dissatisfaction, contempt, and ridicule, more and more strongly expressed. The ridicule and contempt were of course expressed in a respectful form, making it impossible for him to ask wherein he was to blame. They did not talk seriously to him; when reporting to him or asking for his sanction they appeared to be fulfilling a regrettable formality, but they winked behind his back and tried to mislead him at every turn.

Because they could not understand him all these people assumed that it was useless to talk to the old man; that he would never grasp the profundity of their plans, that he would answer with his phrases (which they thought were mere phrases) about a "golden bridge," about the impossibility of crossing the frontier with a crowd of tatterdemalions, and so forth. They had heard all that before. And all he said—that it was necessary to await provisions, or that the men had no boots—was so simple, while what they proposed was so complicated and clever, that it was evident that he was old and stupid and that they, though not in power, were commanders of genius.

After the junction with the army of the brilliant admiral and Petersburg hero Wittgenstein, this mood and the gossip of the staff reached their maximum. Kutúzov saw this and merely sighed and shrugged his shoulders. Only once, after the affair of the Berëzina, did he get angry and write to Bennigsen (who reported separately to the Emperor) the following letter:

"On account of your spells of ill health, will your excellency please be so good as to set off for Kalúga on receipt of this, and there await further commands and appointments from His Imperial Majesty."

But after Bennigsen's departure, the Grand Duke Tsarévich Constantine Pávlovich joined the army. He had taken part in the beginning of the campaign but had subsequently been removed from the army by Kutúzov. Now having come to the army, he informed Kutúzov of the Emperor's displeasure at the poor success of our forces and the slowness of their advance. The Emperor intended to join the army personally in a few days' time.

The old man, experienced in court as well as in military affairs—this same Kutúzov who in August had been chosen commander in chief against the sovereign's wishes and who had removed the Grand Duke and heir-apparent from the army—who on his own authority and contrary to the Emperor's will had decided on the abandonment of Moscow, now realized at once that his day was over, that his part was played, and that the power he was supposed to hold was no longer his. And he understood this not merely from the attitude of the court. He saw on the one hand that the military business in which he had played his part was ended and felt that his mission was accomplished; and at the same time he began to be conscious of the physical weariness of his aged body and of the necessity of physical rest.

On the twenty-ninth of November Kutúzov entered Vílna—his "dear Vílna" as he called it. Twice during his career Kutúzov had been governor of Vílna. In that wealthy town, which had not been injured, he found old friends and associations, besides the comforts of life of which he had so long been deprived. And he suddenly turned from the cares of army and state and, as far as the passions that seethed around him allowed, immersed himself in the quiet life to which he had formerly been accustomed, as if all that was taking place and all that had still to be done in the realm of history did not concern him at all.

Chichagóv, one of the most zealous "cutters-off" and "breakers-up," who had first wanted to effect a diversion in Greece and then in Warsaw but never wished to go where he was sent: Chichagóv, noted for the boldness with which he spoke to the Emperor, and who considered Kutúzov to be under an obligation to him because when he was sent to make peace with Turkey in 1811 independently of Kutúzov, and found that peace had already been concluded, he admitted to the Emperor that the merit of securing that peace was really Kutúzov's; this Chichagóv was the first to meet Kutúzov at the castle where the latter was to stay. In undress naval uniform, with a dirk, and holding his cap under his arm, he handed Kutúzov a garrison report and the keys of the town. The contemptuously respectful attitude of the younger men to the old man in his dotage was expressed in the highest degree by the behavior of Chichagóv, who knew of the accusations that were being directed against Kutúzov.

When speaking to Chichagóv, Kutúzov incidentally mentioned that the vehicles packed with china that had been captured from him at Borísov had been recovered and would be restored to him.

"You mean to imply that I have nothing to eat out of.... On the contrary, I can supply you with everything even if you want to give dinner parties," warmly replied Chichagóv, who tried by every word he spoke to prove his own rectitude and therefore imagined Kutúzov to be animated by the same desire.

Kutúzov, shrugging his shoulders, replied with his subtle penetrating smile: "I meant merely to say what I said."

Contrary to the Emperor's wish Kutúzov detained the greater part of the army at Vílna. Those about him said that he became extraordinarily slack and physically feeble during his stay in that town. He attended to army affairs reluctantly, left everything to his generals, and while awaiting the Emperor's arrival led a dissipated life.

Having left Petersburg on the seventh of December with his suite—Count Tolstóy, Prince Volkónski, Arakchéev, and others—the Emperor reached Vílna on the eleventh, and in his traveling sleigh drove straight to the castle. In spite of the severe frost some hundred generals and staff officers in full parade uniform stood in front of the castle, as well as a guard of honor of the Semënov regiment.

A courier who galloped to the castle in advance, in a troyka with three foam-flecked horses, shouted "Coming!" and Konovnítsyn rushed into the vestibule to inform Kutúzov, who was waiting in the hall porter's little lodge.

A minute later the old man's large stout figure in full-dress uniform, his chest covered with orders and a scarf drawn round his stomach, waddled out into the porch. He put on his hat with its peaks to the sides and, holding his gloves in his hand and walking with an effort sideways down the steps to the level of the street, took in his hand the report he had prepared for the Emperor.

There was running to and fro and whispering; another troyka flew furiously up, and then all eyes were turned on an approaching sleigh in which the figures of the Emperor and Volkónski could already be descried.

From the habit of fifty years all this had a physically agitating effect on the old general. He carefully and hastily felt himself all over, readjusted his hat, and pulling himself together drew himself up and, at the very moment when the Emperor, having alighted from the sleigh, lifted his eyes to him, handed him the report and began speaking in his smooth, ingratiating voice.

The Emperor with a rapid glance scanned Kutúzov from head to foot, frowned for an instant, but immediately mastering himself went up to the old man, extended his arms and embraced him. And this embrace too, owing to a long-standing impression related to his innermost feelings, had its usual effect on Kutúzov and he gave a sob.

The Emperor greeted the officers and the Semënov guard, and again pressing the old man's hand went with him into the castle.

When alone with the field marshal the Emperor expressed his dissatisfaction at the slowness of the pursuit and at the mistakes made at Krásnoe and the Berëzina, and informed him of his intentions for a future campaign abroad. Kutúzov made no rejoinder or remark. The same submissive, expressionless look with which he had listened to the Emperor's commands on the field of Austerlitz seven years before settled on his face now.

When Kutúzov came out of the study and with lowered head was crossing the ballroom with his heavy waddling gait, he was arrested by someone's voice saying:

"Your Serene Highness!"

Kutúzov raised his head and looked for a long while into the eyes of Count Tolstóy, who stood before him holding a silver salver on which lay a small object. Kutúzov seemed not to understand what was expected of him.

Suddenly he seemed to remember; a scarcely perceptible smile flashed across his puffy face, and bowing low and respectfully he took the object that lay on the salver. It was the Order of St. George of the First Class.

CHAPTER XI

Next day the field marshal gave a dinner and ball which the Emperorhonored by his presence. Kutúzov had received the Order of St. George of the First Class and the Emperor showed him the highest honors, but everyone knew of the imperial dissatisfaction with him. The proprieties were observed and the Emperor was the first to set that example, but everybody understood that the old man was blameworthy and good-for-nothing. When Kutúzov, conforming to a custom of Catherine's day, ordered the standards that had been captured to be lowered at the Emperor's feet on his entering the ballroom, the Emperor made a wry face and muttered something in which some people caught the words, "the old comedian."

The Emperor's displeasure with Kutúzov was specially increased at Vílna by the fact that Kutúzov evidently could not or would not understand the importance of the coming campaign.

When on the following morning the Emperor said to the officers assembled about him: "You have not only saved Russia, you have saved Europe!" they all understood that the war was not ended.

Kutúzov alone would not see this and openly expressed his opinion that no fresh war could improve the position or add to the glory of Russia, but could only spoil and lower the glorious position that Russia had gained. He tried to prove to the Emperor the impossibility of levying fresh troops, spoke of the hardships already endured by the people, of the possibility of failure and so forth.

This being the field marshal's frame of mind he was naturally regarded as merely a hindrance and obstacle to the impending war.

To avoid unpleasant encounters with the old man, the natural method was to do what had been done with him at Austerlitz and with Barclay at the beginning of the Russian campaign—to transfer the authority to the Emperor himself, thus cutting the ground from under the commander in chief's feet without upsetting the old man by informing him of the change.

With this object his staff was gradually reconstructed and its real strength removed and transferred to the Emperor. Toll, Konovnítsyn, and Ermólov received fresh appointments. Everyone spoke loudly of the field marshal's great weakness and failing health.

His health had to be bad for his place to be taken away and given to another. And in fact his health was poor.

So naturally, simply, and gradually—just as he had come from Turkey to the Treasury in Petersburg to recruit the militia, and then to the army when he was needed there—now when his part was played out, Kutúzov's place was taken by a new and necessary performer.

The war of 1812, besides its national significance dear to every Russian heart, was now to assume another, a European, significance.

The movement of peoples from west to east was to be succeeded by a movement of peoples from east to west, and for this fresh war another leader was necessary, having qualities and views differing from Kutúzov's and animated by different motives.

Alexander I was as necessary for the movement of the peoples from east to west and for the refixing of national frontiers as Kutúzov had been for the salvation and glory of Russia.

Kutúzov did not understand what Europe, the balance of power, or Napoleon meant. He could not understand it. For the representative of the Russian people, after the enemy had been destroyed and Russia had been liberated and raised to the summit of her glory, there was nothing left to do as a Russian. Nothing remained for the representative of the national war but to die, and Kutúzov died.

CHAPTER XII

As generally happens, Pierre did not feel the full effects of the physical privation and strain he had suffered as prisoner until after they were over. After his liberation he reached Orël, and on the third day there, when preparing to go to Kiev, he fell ill and was laid up for three months. He had what the doctors termed "bilious fever." But despite the fact that the doctors treated him, bled him, and gave him medicines to drink, he recovered.

Scarcely any impression was left on Pierre's mind by all that happened to him from the time of his rescue till his illness. He remembered only the dull gray weather now rainy and now snowy, internal physical distress, and pains in his feet and side. He remembered a general impression of the misfortunes and sufferings of people and of being worried by the curiosity of officers and generals who questioned him, he also remembered his difficulty in procuring a conveyance and horses, and above all he remembered his incapacity to think and feel all that time. On the day of his rescue he had seen the body of PétyaRostóv. That same day he had learned that Prince Andrew, after surviving the battle of Borodinó for more than a month had recently died in the Rostóvs' house at Yaroslávl, and Denísov who told him this news also mentioned Hélène's death, supposing that Pierre had heard of it long before. All this at the time seemed merely strange to Pierre: he felt he could not grasp its significance. Just then he was only anxious to get away as quickly as possible from places where people were killing one another, to some peaceful refuge where he could recover himself, rest, and think over all the strange new facts he had learned; but on reaching Orël he immediately fell ill. When he came to himself after his illness he saw in attendance on him two of his servants, Terénty and Váska, who had come from Moscow; and also his cousin the eldest princess, who had been living on his estate at Eléts and hearing of his rescue and illness had come to look after him.

It was only gradually during his convalescence that Pierre lost the impressions he had become accustomed to during the last few months and got used to the idea that no one would oblige him to go anywhere tomorrow, that no one would deprive him of his warm bed, and that he would be sure to get his dinner, tea, and supper. But for a long time in his dreams he still saw himself in the conditions of captivity. In the same way little by little he came to understand the news he had been told after his rescue, about the death of Prince Andrew, the death of his wife, and the destruction of the French.

A joyous feeling of freedom—that complete inalienable freedom natural to man which he had first experienced at the first halt outside Moscow—filled Pierre's soul during his convalescence. He was surprised to find that this inner freedom, which was independent of external conditions, now had as it were an additional setting of external liberty. He was alone in a strange town, without acquaintances. No one demanded anything of him or sent him anywhere. He had all he wanted: the thought of his wife which had been a continual torment to him was no longer there, since she was no more.

"Oh, how good! How splendid!" said he to himself when a cleanly laid table was moved up to him with savory beef tea, or when he lay down for the night on a soft clean bed, or when he remembered that the French had gone and that his wife was no more. "Oh, how good, how splendid!"

And by old habit he asked himself the question: "Well, and what then? What am I going to do?" And he immediately gave himself the answer: "Well, I shall live. Ah, how splendid!"

The very question that had formerly tormented him, the thing he had continually sought to find—the aim of life—no longer existed for him now. That search for the aim of life had not merely disappeared temporarily—he felt that it no longer existed for him and could not present itself again. And this very absence of an aim gave him the complete, joyous sense of freedom which constituted his happiness at this time.

He could not see an aim, for he now had faith—not faith in any kind of rule, or words, or ideas, but faith in an ever-living, ever-manifest God. Formerly he had sought Him in aims he set himself. That search for an aim had been simply a search for God, and suddenly in his captivity he had learned not by words or reasoning but by direct feeling what his nurse had told him long ago: that God is here and everywhere. In his captivity he had learned that in Karatáev God was greater, more infinite and unfathomable than in the Architect of the Universe recognized by the Freemasons. He felt like a man who after straining his eyes to see into the far distance finds what he sought at his very feet. All his life he had looked over the heads of the men around him, when he should have merely looked in front of him without straining his eyes.

In the past he had never been able to find that great inscrutable infinite *something*. He had only felt that it must exist somewhere and had looked for it. In everything near and comprehensible he had seen only what was limited, petty, commonplace, and senseless. He had equipped himself with a mental telescope and looked into remote space, where petty worldliness hiding itself in misty distance had seemed to him great and infinite merely because it was not clearly seen. And such had European life, politics, Freemasonry, philosophy, and philanthropy seemed to him. But even then, at moments of weakness as he had accounted them, his mind had penetrated to those distances and he had there seen the same pettiness, worldliness, and senselessness. Now, however, he had learned to see the great, eternal, and infinite in everything, and therefore—to see it and enjoy its contemplation—he naturally threw away the telescope through which he had till now gazed over men's heads, and gladly regarded the ever-changing, eternally great, unfathomable, and infinite life around him. And the closer he looked the more tranquil and happy he became. That dreadful question, "What for?" which had formerly destroyed all his mental edifices, no longer existed for him. To that question, "What for?" a simple answer was now always ready in his soul: "Because there is a God, that God without whose will not one hair falls from a man's head."

CHAPTER XIII

In external ways Pierre had hardly changed at all. In appearance he was just what he used to be. As before he was absent-minded and seemed occupied not with what was before his eyes but with something special of his own. The difference between his former and present self was that formerly when he did not grasp what lay before him or was said to him, he had puckered his forehead painfully as if vainly seeking to distinguish something at a distance. At present he still forgot what was said to him and still did not see what was before his eyes, but he now looked with a scarcely perceptible and seemingly ironic smile at what was before him and listened to what was said, though evidently seeing and hearing something quite different. Formerly he had appeared to be a kindhearted but unhappy man, and so people had been inclined to avoid him. Now a smile at the joy of life always played round his lips, and sympathy for others shone in his eyes with a questioning look as to whether they were as contented as he was, and people felt pleased by his presence.

Previously he had talked a great deal, grew excited when he talked, and seldom listened; now he was seldom carried away in conversation and knew how to listen so that people readily told him their most intimate secrets.

The princess, who had never liked Pierre and had been particularly hostile to him since she had felt herself under obligations to him after the old count's death, now after staying a short time in Orël—where she had come intending to show Pierre that in spite of his ingratitude she considered it her duty to nurse him—felt to her surprise and vexation that she had become fond of him. Pierre did not in any way seek her approval, he merely studied her with interest. Formerly she had felt that he regarded her with indifference and irony, and so had shrunk into herself as she did with others and had shown him only the combative side of her nature; but now he seemed to be trying to understand the most intimate places of her heart, and, mistrustfully at first but afterwards gratefully, she let him see the hidden, kindly sides of her character.

The most cunning man could not have crept into her confidence more successfully, evoking memories of the best times of her youth and showing sympathy with them. Yet Pierre's cunning consisted simply in finding pleasure in drawing out the human qualities of the embittered, hard, and (in her own way) proud princess.

"Yes, he is a very, very kind man when he is not under the influence of bad people but of people such as myself," thought she.

His servants too—Terénty and Váska—in their own way noticed the change that had taken place in Pierre. They considered that he had become much "simpler." Terénty, when he had helped him undress and wished him good night, often lingered with his master's boots in his hands and clothes over his arm, to see whether he would not start a talk. And Pierre, noticing that Terénty wanted a chat, generally kept him there.

"Well, tell me... now, how did you get food?" he would ask.

And Terénty would begin talking of the destruction of Moscow, and of the old count, and would stand for a long time holding the clothes and talking, or sometimes listening to Pierre's stories, and then would go out into the hall with a pleasant sense of intimacy with his master and affection for him.

The doctor who attended Pierre and visited him every day, though he considered it his duty as a doctor to pose as a man whose every moment was of value to suffering humanity, would sit for hours with Pierre telling him his favorite anecdotes and his observations on the characters of his patients in general, and especially of the ladies.

"It's a pleasure to talk to a man like that; he is not like our provincials," he would say.

There were several prisoners from the French army in Orël, and the doctor brought one of them, a young Italian, to see Pierre.

This officer began visiting Pierre, and the princess used to make fun of the tenderness the Italian expressed for him.

The Italian seemed happy only when he could come to see Pierre, talk with him, tell him about his past, his life at home, and his love, and pour out to him his indignation against the French and especially against Napoleon.

"If all Russians are in the least like you, it is sacrilege to fight such a nation," he said to Pierre. "You, who have suffered so from the French, do not even feel animosity toward them."

Pierre had evoked the passionate affection of the Italian merely by evoking the best side of his nature and taking a pleasure in so doing.

During the last days of Pierre's stay in Orël his old Masonic acquaintance Count Willarski, who had introduced him to the lodge in 1807, came to see him. Willarski was married to a Russian heiress who had a large estate in Orël province, and he occupied a temporary post in the commissariat department in that town.

Hearing that Bezúkhov was in Orël, Willarski, though they had never been intimate, came to him with the professions of friendship and intimacy that people who meet in a desert generally express for one another. Willarski felt dull in Orël and was pleased to meet a man of his own circle and, as he supposed, of similar interests.

But to his surprise Willarski soon noticed that Pierre had lagged much behind the times, and had sunk, as he expressed it to himself, into apathy and egotism.

"You are letting yourself go, my dear fellow," he said.

But for all that Willarski found it pleasanter now than it had been formerly to be with Pierre, and came to see him every day. To Pierre as he looked at and listened to Willarski, it seemed strange to think that he had been like that himself but a short time before.

Willarski was a married man with a family, busy with his family affairs, his wife's affairs, and his official duties. He regarded all these occupations as hindrances to life, and considered that they were all contemptible because their aim was the welfare of himself and his family. Military, administrative, political, and Masonic interests continually absorbed his attention. And Pierre, without trying to change the other's views and without condemning him, but with the quiet, joyful, and amused smile now habitual to him, was interested in this strange though very familiar phenomenon.

There was a new feature in Pierre's relations with Willarski, with the princess, with the doctor, and with all the people he now met, which gained for him the general good will. This was his acknowledgment of the impossibility of changing a man's convictions by words, and his recognition of the possibility of everyone thinking, feeling, and seeing things each from his own point of view. This legitimate peculiarity of each individual which used to excite and irritate Pierre now became a basis of the sympathy he felt for, and the interest he took in, other people. The difference, and sometimes complete contradiction, between men's opinions and their lives, and between one man and another, pleased him and drew from him an amused and gentle smile.

In practical matters Pierre unexpectedly felt within himself a center of gravity he had previously lacked. Formerly all pecuniary questions, especially requests for money to which, as an extremely wealthy man, he was very exposed, produced in him a state of hopeless agitation and perplexity. "To give or not to give?" he had asked himself. "I have it and he needs it. But someone else needs it still more. Who needs it most? And perhaps they are both impostors?" In the old days he had been unable to find a way out of all these surmises and had given to all who asked as long as he had anything to give. Formerly he had been in a similar state of perplexity with regard to every question concerning his property, when one person advised one thing and another something else.

Now to his surprise he found that he no longer felt either doubt or perplexity about these questions. There was now within him a judge who by some rule unknown to him decided what should or should not be done.

He was as indifferent as heretofore to money matters, but now he felt certain of what ought and what ought not to be done. The first time he had recourse to his new judge was when a French prisoner, a colonel, came to him and, after talking a great deal about his exploits, concluded by making what amounted to a demand that Pierre should give him four thousand francs to send to his wife and children. Pierre refused without the least difficulty or effort, and was afterwards surprised how simple and easy had been what used to appear so insurmountably difficult. At the same time that he refused the colonel's demand he made up his mind that he must have recourse to artifice when leaving Orël, to induce the Italian officer to accept some money of which he was evidently in need. A further proof to Pierre of his own more settled outlook on practical matters was furnished by his decision with regard to his wife's debts and to the rebuilding of his houses in and near Moscow.

His head steward came to him at Orël and Pierre reckoned up with him his diminished income. The burning of Moscow had cost him, according to the head steward's calculation, about two million rubles.

To console Pierre for these losses the head steward gave him an estimate showing that despite these losses his income would not be diminished but would even be increased if he refused to pay his wife's debts which he was under no obligation to meet, and did not rebuild his Moscow house and the country house on his Moscow estate, which had cost him eighty thousand rubles a year and brought in nothing.

"Yes, of course that's true," said Pierre with a cheerful smile. "I don't need all that at all. By being ruined I have become much richer."

But in January Savélich came from Moscow and gave him an account of the state of things there, and spoke of the estimate an architect had made of the cost of rebuilding the town and country houses, speaking of this as of a settled matter. About the same time he received letters from Prince Vasíli and other Petersburg acquaintances speaking of his wife's debts. And Pierre decided that the steward's proposals which had so pleased him were wrong and that he must go to Petersburg and settle his wife's affairs and must rebuild in Moscow. Why this was necessary he did not know, but he knew for certain that it was necessary. His income would be reduced by three fourths, but he felt it must be done.

Willarski was going to Moscow and they agreed to travel together.

During the whole time of his convalescence in Orël Pierre had experienced a feeling of joy, freedom, and life; but when during his journey he found himself in the open world and saw hundreds of new faces, that feeling was intensified. Throughout his journey he felt like a schoolboy on holiday. Everyone—the stagecoach driver, the post-house overseers, the peasants on the roads and in the villages—had a new significance for him. The presence and remarks of Willarski who continually deplored the ignorance and poverty of Russia and its backwardness compared with Europe only heightened Pierre's pleasure. Where Willarski saw deadness Pierre saw an extraordinary strength and vitality—the strength which in that vast space amid the snows maintained the life of this original, peculiar, and unique people. He did not contradict Willarski and even seemed to agree with him—an apparent agreement being the simplest way to avoid discussions that could lead to nothing—and he smiled joyfully as he listened to him.

CHAPTER XIV

It would be difficult to explain why and whither ants whose heap has been destroyed are hurrying: some from the heap dragging bits of rubbish, larvae, and corpses, others back to the heap, or why they jostle, overtake one another, and fight, and it would be equally difficult to explain what caused the Russians after the departure of the French to throng to the place that had formerly been Moscow. But when we watch the ants round their ruined heap, the tenacity, energy, and immense number of the delving insects prove that despite the destruction of the heap, something indestructible, which though intangible is the real strength of the colony, still exists; and similarly, though in Moscow in the month of October there was no government and no churches, shrines, riches, or houses—it was still the Moscow it had been in August. All was destroyed, except something intangible yet powerful and indestructible.

The motives of those who thronged from all sides to Moscow after it had been cleared of the enemy were most diverse and personal, and at first for the most part savage and brutal. One motive only they all had in common: a desire to get to the place that had been called Moscow, to apply their activities there.

Within a week Moscow already had fifteen thousand inhabitants, in a fortnight twenty-five thousand, and so on. By the autumn of 1813 the number, ever increasing and increasing, exceeded what it had been in 1812.

The first Russians to enter Moscow were the Cossacks of Wintzingerode's detachment, peasants from the adjacent villages, and residents who had fled from Moscow and had been hiding in its vicinity. The Russians who entered Moscow, finding it plundered, plundered it in their turn. They continued what the French had begun. Trains of peasant carts came to Moscow to carry off to the villages what had been abandoned in the ruined houses and the streets. The Cossacks carried off what they could to their camps, and the householders seized all they could find in other houses and moved it to their own, pretending that it was their property.

But the first plunderers were followed by a second and a third contingent, and with increasing numbers plundering became more and more difficult and assumed more definite forms.

The French found Moscow abandoned but with all the organizations of regular life, with diverse branches of commerce and craftsmanship, with luxury, and governmental and religious institutions. These forms were lifeless but still existed. There were bazaars, shops, warehouses, market stalls, granaries—for the most part still stocked with goods—and there were factories and workshops, palaces and wealthy houses filled with luxuries, hospitals, prisons, government offices, churches, and cathedrals. The longer the French remained the more these forms of town life perished, until finally all was merged into one confused, lifeless scene of plunder.

The more the plundering by the French continued, the more both the wealth of Moscow and the strength of its plunderers was destroyed. But plundering by the Russians, with which the reoccupation of the city began, had an opposite effect: the longer it continued and the greater the number of people taking part in it the more rapidly was the wealth of the city and its regular life restored.

Besides the plunderers, very various people, some drawn by curiosity, some by official duties, some by self-interest—house owners, clergy, officials of all kinds, tradesmen, artisans, and peasants—streamed into Moscow as blood flows to the heart.

Within a week the peasants who came with empty carts to carry off plunder were stopped by the authorities and made to cart the corpses out of the town. Other peasants, having heard of their comrades' discomfiture, came to town bringing rye, oats, and hay, and beat down one another's prices to below what they had been in former days. Gangs of carpenters hoping for high pay arrived in Moscow every day, and on all sides logs were being hewn, new houses built, and old, charred ones repaired. Tradesmen began trading in booths. Cookshops and taverns were opened in partially burned houses. The clergy resumed the services in many churches that had not been burned. Donors contributed Church property that had been stolen. Government clerks set up their baize-covered tables and their pigeonholes of documents in small rooms. The higher authorities and the police organized the distribution of goods left behind by the French. The owners of houses in which much property had been left, brought there from other houses, complained of the injustice of taking everything to the Faceted Palace in the Krémlin; others insisted that as the French had gathered things from different houses into this or that house, it would be unfair to allow its owner to keep all that was found there. They abused the police and bribed them, made out estimates at ten times their value for government stores that had perished in the fire, and demanded relief. And Count Rostopchín wrote proclamations.

CHAPTER XV

At the end of January Pierre went to Moscow and stayed in an annex of his house which had not been burned. He called on Count Rostopchín and on some acquaintances who were back in Moscow, and he intended to leave for Petersburg two days later. Everybody was celebrating the victory, everything was bubbling with life in the ruined but reviving city. Everyone was pleased to see Pierre, everyone wished to meet him, and everyone questioned him about what he had seen. Pierre felt particularly well disposed toward them all, but was now instinctively on his guard for fear of binding himself in any way. To all questions put to him—whether important or quite trifling—such as: Where would he live? Was he going to rebuild? When was he going to Petersburg and would he mind taking a parcel for someone?—he replied: "Yes, perhaps," or, "I think so," and so on.

He had heard that the Rostóvs were at Kostromá but the thought of Natásha seldom occurred to him. If it did it was only as a pleasant memory of the distant past. He felt himself not only free from social obligations but also from that feeling which, it seemed to him, he had aroused in himself.

On the third day after his arrival he heard from the Drubetskóys that Princess Mary was in Moscow. The death, sufferings, and last days of Prince Andrew had often occupied Pierre's thoughts and now recurred to him with fresh vividness. Having heard at dinner that Princess Mary was in Moscow and living in her house—which had not been burned—in Vozdvízhenka Street, he drove that same evening to see her.

On his way to the house Pierre kept thinking of Prince Andrew, of their friendship, of his various meetings with him, and especially of the last one at Borodinó.

"Is it possible that he died in the bitter frame of mind he was then in? Is it possible that the meaning of life was not disclosed to him before he died?" thought Pierre. He recalled Karatáev and his death and involuntarily began to compare these two men, so different, and yet so similar in that they had both lived and both died and in the love he felt for both of them.

Pierre drove up to the house of the old prince in a most serious mood. The house had escaped the fire; it showed signs of damage but its general aspect was unchanged. The old footman, who met Pierre with a stern face as if wishing to make the visitor feel that the absence of the old prince had not disturbed the order of things in the house, informed him that the princess had gone to her own apartments, and that she received on Sundays.

"Announce me. Perhaps she will see me," said Pierre.

"Yes, sir," said the man. "Please step into the portrait gallery."

A few minutes later the footman returned with Dessalles, who brought word from the princess that she would be very glad to see Pierre if he would excuse her want of ceremony and come upstairs to her apartment.

In a rather low room lit by one candle sat the princess and with her another person dressed in black. Pierre remembered that the princess always had lady companions, but who they were and what they were like he never knew or remembered. "This must be one of her companions," he thought, glancing at the lady in the black dress.

The princess rose quickly to meet him and held out her hand.

"Yes," she said, looking at his altered face after he had kissed her hand, "so this is how we meet again. He spoke of you even at the very last," she went on, turning her eyes from Pierre to her companion with a shyness that surprised him for an instant.

"I was so glad to hear of your safety. It was the first piece of good news we had received for a long time."

Again the princess glanced round at her companion with even more uneasiness in her manner and was about to add something, but Pierre interrupted her.

"Just imagine—I knew nothing about him!" said he. "I thought he had been killed. All I know I heard at second hand from others. I only know that he fell in with the Rostóvs.... What a strange coincidence!"

Pierre spoke rapidly and with animation. He glanced once at the companion's face, saw her attentive and kindly gaze fixed on him, and, as often happens when one is talking, felt somehow that this companion in the black dress was a good, kind, excellent creature who would not hinder his conversing freely with Princess Mary.

But when he mentioned the Rostóvs, Princess Mary's face expressed still greater embarrassment. She again glanced rapidly from Pierre's face to that of the lady in the black dress and said:

"Do you really not recognize her?"

Pierre looked again at the companion's pale, delicate face with its black eyes and peculiar mouth, and something near to him, long forgotten and more than sweet, looked at him from those attentive eyes.

"But no, it can't be!" he thought. "This stern, thin, pale face that looks so much older! It cannot be she. It merely reminds me of her." But at that moment Princess Mary said, "Natásha!" And with difficulty, effort, and stress, like the opening of a door grown rusty on its hinges, a smile appeared on the face with the attentive eyes, and from that opening door came a breath of fragrance which suffused Pierre with a happiness he had long forgotten and of which he had not even been thinking—especially at that moment. It suffused him, seized him, and enveloped him completely. When she smiled doubt was no longer possible, it was Natásha and he loved her.

At that moment Pierre involuntarily betrayed to her, to Princess Mary, and above all to himself, a secret of which he himself had been unaware. He flushed joyfully yet with painful distress. He tried to hide his agitation. But the more he tried to hide it the more clearly—clearer than any words could have done—did he betray to himself, to her, and to Princess Mary that he loved her.

"No, it's only the unexpectedness of it," thought Pierre. But as soon as he tried to continue the conversation he had begun with Princess Mary he again glanced at Natásha, and a still-deeper flush suffused his face and a still-stronger agitation of mingled joy and fear seized his soul. He became confused in his speech and stopped in the middle of what he was saying.

Pierre had failed to notice Natásha because he did not at all expect to see her there, but he had failed to recognize her because the change in her since he last saw her was immense. She had grown thin and pale, but that was not what made her unrecognizable; she was unrecognizable at the moment he entered because on that face whose eyes had always shone with a suppressed smile of the joy of life, now when he first entered and glanced at her there was not the least shadow of a smile: only her eyes were kindly attentive and sadly interrogative.

Pierre's confusion was not reflected by any confusion on Natásha's part, but only by the pleasure that just perceptibly lit up her whole face.

CHAPTER XVI

"She has come to stay with me," said Princess Mary. "The count and countess will be here in a few days. The countess is in a dreadful state; but it was necessary for Natásha herself to see a doctor. They insisted on her coming with me."

"Yes, is there a family free from sorrow now?" said Pierre, addressing Natásha. "You know it happened the very day we were rescued. I saw him. What a delightful boy he was!"

Natásha looked at him, and by way of answer to his words her eyes widened and lit up.

"What can one say or think of as a consolation?" said Pierre. "Nothing! Why had such a splendid boy, so full of life, to die?"

"Yes, in these days it would be hard to live without faith..." remarked Princess Mary.

"Yes, yes, that is really true," Pierre hastily interrupted her.

"Why is it true?" Natásha asked, looking attentively into Pierre's eyes.

"How can you ask why?" said Princess Mary. "The thought alone of what awaits..."

Natásha without waiting for Princess Mary to finish again looked inquiringly at Pierre.

"And because," Pierre continued, "only one who believes that there is a God ruling us can bear a loss such as hers and... yours."

Natásha had already opened her mouth to speak but suddenly stopped. Pierre hurriedly turned away from her and again addressed Princess Mary, asking about his friend's last days.

Pierre's confusion had now almost vanished, but at the same time he felt that his freedom had also completely gone. He felt that there was now a judge of his every word and action whose judgment mattered more to him than that of all the rest of the world. As he spoke now he was considering what impression his words would make on Natásha. He did not purposely say things to please her, but whatever he was saying he regarded from her standpoint.

Princess Mary—reluctantly as is usual in such cases—began telling of the condition in which she had found Prince Andrew. But Pierre's face quivering with emotion, his questions and his eager restless expression, gradually compelled her to go into details which she feared to recall for her own sake.

"Yes, yes, and so...?" Pierre kept saying as he leaned toward her with his whole body and eagerly listened to her story. "Yes, yes... so he grew tranquil and softened? With all his soul he had always sought one thing—to be perfectly good—so he could not be afraid of death. The faults he had—if he had any—were not of his making. So he did soften?... What a happy thing that he saw you again," he added, suddenly turning to Natásha and looking at her with eyes full of tears.

Natásha's face twitched. She frowned and lowered her eyes for a moment. She hesitated for an instant whether to speak or not.

"Yes, that was happiness," she then said in her quiet voice with its deep chest notes. "For me it certainly was happiness." She paused. "And he... he... he said he was wishing for it at the very moment I entered the room...."

Natásha's voice broke. She blushed, pressed her clasped hands on her knees, and then controlling herself with an evident effort lifted her head and began to speak rapidly.

"We knew nothing of it when we started from Moscow. I did not dare to ask about him. Then suddenly Sónya told me he was traveling with us. I had no idea and could not imagine what state he was in, all I wanted was to see him and be with him," she said, trembling, and breathing quickly.

And not letting them interrupt her she went on to tell what she had never yet mentioned to anyone—all she had lived through during those three weeks of their journey and life at Yaroslávl.

Pierre listened to her with lips parted and eyes fixed upon her full of tears. As he listened he did not think of Prince Andrew, nor of death, nor of what she was telling. He listened to her and felt only pity for her, for what she was suffering now while she was speaking.

Princess Mary, frowning in her effort to hold back her tears, sat beside Natásha, and heard for the first time the story of those last days of her brother's and Natásha's love.

Evidently Natásha needed to tell that painful yet joyful tale.

She spoke, mingling most trifling details with the intimate secrets of her soul, and it seemed as if she could never finish. Several times she repeated the same thing twice.

Dessalles' voice was heard outside the door asking whether little Nicholas might come in to say good night.

"Well, that's all—everything," said Natásha.

She got up quickly just as Nicholas entered, almost ran to the door which was hidden by curtains, struck her head against it, and rushed from the room with a moan either of pain or sorrow.

Pierre gazed at the door through which she had disappeared and did not understand why he suddenly felt all alone in the world.

Princess Mary roused him from his abstraction by drawing his attention to her nephew who had entered the room.

At that moment of emotional tenderness young Nicholas' face, which resembled his father's, affected Pierre so much that when he had kissed the boy he got up quickly, took out his handkerchief, and went to the window. He wished to take leave of Princess Mary, but she would not let him go.

"No, Natásha and I sometimes don't go to sleep till after two, so please don't go. I will order supper. Go downstairs, we will come immediately."

Before Pierre left the room Princess Mary told him: "This is the first time she has talked of him like that."

CHAPTER XVII

Pierre was shown into the large, brightly lit dining room; a few minutes later he heard footsteps and Princess Mary entered with Natásha. Natásha was calm, though a severe and grave expression had again settled on her face. They all three of them now experienced that feeling of awkwardness which usually follows after a serious and heartfelt talk. It is impossible to go back to the same conversation, to talk of trifles is awkward, and yet the desire to speak is there and silence seems like affectation. They went silently to table. The footmen drew back the chairs and pushed them up again. Pierre unfolded his cold table napkin and, resolving to break the silence, looked at Natásha and at Princess Mary. They had evidently both formed the same resolution; the eyes of both shone with satisfaction and a confession that besides sorrow life also has joy.

"Do you take vodka, Count?" asked Princess Mary, and those words suddenly banished the shadows of the past. "Now tell us about yourself," said she. "One hears such improbable wonders about you."

"Yes," replied Pierre with the smile of mild irony now habitual to him. "They even tell me wonders I myself never dreamed of! Mary Abrámovna invited me to her house and kept telling me what had happened, or ought to have happened, to me. StepánStepánych also instructed me how I ought to tell of my experiences. In general I have noticed that it is very easy to be an interesting man (I am an interesting man now); people invite me out and tell me all about myself."

Natásha smiled and was on the point of speaking.

"We have been told," Princess Mary interrupted her, "that you lost two millions in Moscow. Is that true?"

"But I am three times as rich as before," returned Pierre.

Though the position was now altered by his decision to pay his wife's debts and to rebuild his houses, Pierre still maintained that he had become three times as rich as before.

"What I have certainly gained is freedom," he began seriously, but did not continue, noticing that this theme was too egotistic.

"And are you building?"

"Yes. Savélich says I must!"

"Tell me, you did not know of the countess' death when you decided to remain in Moscow?" asked Princess Mary and immediately blushed, noticing that her question, following his mention of freedom, ascribed to his words a meaning he had perhaps not intended.

"No," answered Pierre, evidently not considering awkward the meaning Princess Mary had given to his words. "I heard of it in Orël and you cannot imagine how it shocked me. We were not an exemplary couple," he added quickly, glancing at Natásha and noticing on her face curiosity as to how he would speak of his wife, "but her death shocked me terribly. When two people quarrel they are always both in fault, and one's own guilt suddenly becomes terribly serious when the other is no longer alive. And then such a death... without friends and without consolation! I am very, very sorry for her," he concluded, and was pleased to notice a look of glad approval on Natásha's face.

"Yes, and so you are once more an eligible bachelor," said Princess Mary.

Pierre suddenly flushed crimson and for a long time tried not to look at Natásha. When he ventured to glance her way again her face was cold, stern, and he fancied even contemptuous.

"And did you really see and speak to Napoleon, as we have been told?" said Princess Mary.

Pierre laughed.

"No, not once! Everybody seems to imagine that being taken prisoner means being Napoleon's guest. Not only did I never see him but I heard nothing about him—I was in much lower company!"

Supper was over, and Pierre who at first declined to speak about his captivity was gradually led on to do so.

"But it's true that you remained in Moscow to kill Napoleon?" Natásha asked with a slight smile. "I guessed it then when we met at the Súkharev tower, do you remember?"

Pierre admitted that it was true, and from that was gradually led by Princess Mary's questions and especially by Natásha's into giving a detailed account of his adventures.

At first he spoke with the amused and mild irony now customary with him toward everybody and especially toward himself, but when he came to describe the horrors and sufferings he had witnessed he was unconsciously carried away and began speaking with the suppressed emotion of a man re-experiencing in recollection strong impressions he has lived through.

Princess Mary with a gentle smile looked now at Pierre and now at Natásha. In the whole narrative she saw only Pierre and his goodness. Natásha, leaning on her elbow, the expression of her face constantly changing with the narrative, watched Pierre with an attention that never wandered—evidently herself experiencing all that he described. Not only her look, but her exclamations and the brief questions she put, showed Pierre that she understood just what he wished to convey. It was clear that she understood not only what he said but also what he wished to, but could not, express in words. The account Pierre gave of the incident with the child and the woman for protecting whom he was arrested was this: "It was an awful sight—children abandoned, some in the flames... One was snatched out before my eyes... and there were women who had their things snatched off and their earrings torn out..." he flushed and grew confused. "Then a patrol arrived and all the men—all those who were not looting, that is—were arrested, and I among them."

"I am sure you're not telling us everything; I am sure you did something..." said Natásha and pausing added, "something fine?"

Pierre continued. When he spoke of the execution he wanted to pass over the horrible details, but Natásha insisted that he should not omit anything.

Pierre began to tell about Karatáev, but paused. By this time he had risen from the table and was pacing the room, Natásha following him with her eyes. Then he added:

"No, you can't understand what I learned from that illiterate man—that simple fellow."

"Yes, yes, go on!" said Natásha. "Where is he?"

"They killed him almost before my eyes."

And Pierre, his voice trembling continually, went on to tell of the last days of their retreat, of Karatáev's illness and his death.

He told of his adventures as he had never yet recalled them. He now, as it were, saw a new meaning in all he had gone through. Now that he was telling it all to Natásha he experienced that pleasure which a man has when women listen to him—not clever women who when listening either try to remember what they hear to enrich their minds and when opportunity offers to retell it, or who wish to adopt it to some thought of their own and promptly contribute their own clever comments prepared in their little mental workshop—but the pleasure given by real women gifted with a capacity to select and absorb the very best a man shows of himself. Natásha without knowing it was all attention: she did not lose a word, no single quiver in Pierre's voice, no look, no twitch of a muscle in his face, nor a single gesture. She caught the unfinished word in its flight and took it straight into her open heart, divining the secret meaning of all Pierre's mental travail.

Princess Mary understood his story and sympathized with him, but she now saw something else that absorbed all her attention. She saw the possibility of love and happiness between Natásha and Pierre, and the first thought of this filled her heart with gladness.

It was three o'clock in the morning. The footmen came in with sad and stern faces to change the candles, but no one noticed them.

Pierre finished his story. Natásha continued to look at him intently with bright, attentive, and animated eyes, as if trying to understand something more which he had perhaps left untold. Pierre in shamefaced and happy confusion glanced occasionally at her, and tried to think what to say next to introduce a fresh subject. Princess Mary was silent. It occurred to none of them that it was three o'clock and time to go to bed.

"People speak of misfortunes and sufferings," remarked Pierre, "but if at this moment I were asked: 'Would you rather be what you were before you were taken prisoner, or go through all this again?' then for heaven's sake let me again have captivity and horseflesh! We imagine that when we are thrown out of our usual ruts all is lost, but it is only then that what is new and good begins. While there is life there is happiness. There is much, much before us. I say this to you," he added, turning to Natásha.

"Yes, yes," she said, answering something quite different. "I too should wish nothing but to relive it all from the beginning."

Pierre looked intently at her.

"Yes, and nothing more," said Natásha.

"It's not true, not true!" cried Pierre. "I am not to blame for being alive and wishing to live—nor you either."

Suddenly Natásha bent her head, covered her face with her hands, and began to cry.

"What is it, Natásha?" said Princess Mary.

"Nothing, nothing." She smiled at Pierre through her tears. "Good night! It is time for bed."

Pierre rose and took his leave.

Princess Mary and Natásha met as usual in the bedroom. They talked of what Pierre had told them. Princess Mary did not express her opinion of Pierre nor did Natásha speak of him.

"Well, good night, Mary!" said Natásha. "Do you know, I am often afraid that by not speaking of him" (she meant Prince Andrew) "for fear of not doing justice to our feelings, we forget him."

Princess Mary sighed deeply and thereby acknowledged the justice of Natásha's remark, but she did not express agreement in words.

"Is it possible to forget?" said she.

"It did me so much good to tell all about it today. It was hard and painful, but good, very good!" said Natásha. "I am sure he really loved him. That is why I told him... Was it all right?" she added, suddenly blushing.

"To tell Pierre? Oh, yes. What a splendid man he is!" said Princess Mary.

"Do you know, Mary..." Natásha suddenly said with a mischievous smile such as Princess Mary had not seen on her face for a long time, "he has somehow grown so clean, smooth, and fresh—as if he had just come out of a Russian bath; do you understand? Out of a moral bath. Isn't it true?"

"Yes," replied Princess Mary. "He has greatly improved."

"With a short coat and his hair cropped; just as if, well, just as if he had come straight from the bath... Papa used to..."

"I understand why *he*" (Prince Andrew) "liked no one so much as him," said Princess Mary.

"Yes, and yet he is quite different. They say men are friends when they are quite different. That must be true. Really he is quite unlike him—in everything."

"Yes, but he's wonderful."

"Well, good night," said Natásha.

And the same mischievous smile lingered for a long time on her face as if it had been forgotten there.

CHAPTER XVIII

It was a long time before Pierre could fall asleep that night. He paced up and down his room, now turning his thoughts on a difficult problem and frowning, now suddenly shrugging his shoulders and wincing, and now smiling happily.

He was thinking of Prince Andrew, of Natásha, and of their love, at one moment jealous of her past, then reproaching himself for that feeling. It was already six in the morning and he still paced up and down the room.

"Well, what's to be done if it cannot be avoided? What's to be done? Evidently it has to be so," said he to himself, and hastily undressing he got into bed, happy and agitated but free from hesitation or indecision.

"Strange and impossible as such happiness seems, I must do everything that she and I may be man and wife," he told himself.

A few days previously Pierre had decided to go to Petersburg on the Friday. When he awoke on the Thursday, Savélich came to ask him about packing for the journey.

"What, to Petersburg? What is Petersburg? Who is there in Petersburg?" he asked involuntarily, though only to himself. "Oh, yes, long ago before this happened I did for some reason mean to go to Petersburg," he reflected. "Why? But perhaps I shall go. What a good fellow he is and how attentive, and how he remembers everything," he thought, looking at Savélich's old face, "and what a pleasant smile he has!"

"Well, Savélich, do you still not wish to accept your freedom?" Pierre asked him.

"What's the good of freedom to me, your excellency? We lived under the late count—the kingdom of heaven be his!—and we have lived under you too, without ever being wronged."

"And your children?"

"The children will live just the same. With such masters one can live."

"But what about my heirs?" said Pierre. "Supposing I suddenly marry... it might happen," he added with an involuntary smile.

"If I may take the liberty, your excellency, it would be a good thing."

"How easy he thinks it," thought Pierre. "He doesn't know how terrible it is and how dangerous. Too soon or too late... it is terrible!"

"So what are your orders? Are you starting tomorrow?" asked Savélich.

"No, I'll put it off for a bit. I'll tell you later. You must forgive the trouble I have put you to," said Pierre, and seeing Savélich smile, he thought: "But how strange it is that he should not know that now there is no Petersburg for me, and that *that* must be settled first of all! But probably he knows it well enough and is only pretending. Shall I have a talk with him and see what he thinks?" Pierre reflected. "No, another time."

At breakfast Pierre told the princess, his cousin, that he had been to see Princess Mary the day before and had there met—"Whom do you think? NatáshaRostóva!"

The princess seemed to see nothing more extraordinary in that than if he had seen Anna Semënovna.

"Do you know her?" asked Pierre.

"I have seen the princess," she replied. "I heard that they were arranging a match for her with young Rostóv. It would be a very good thing for the Rostóvs, they are said to be utterly ruined."

"No; I mean do you know NatáshaRostóva?"

"I heard about that affair of hers at the time. It was a great pity."

"No, she either doesn't understand or is pretending," thought Pierre. "Better not say anything to her either."

The princess too had prepared provisions for Pierre's journey.

"How kind they all are," thought Pierre. "What is surprising is that they should trouble about these things now when it can no longer be of interest to them. And all for me!"

On the same day the Chief of Police came to Pierre, inviting him to send a representative to the Faceted Palace to recover things that were to be returned to their owners that day.

"And this man too," thought Pierre, looking into the face of the Chief of Police. "What a fine, good-looking officer and how kind. Fancy bothering about such trifles *now!* And they actually say he is not honest and takes bribes. What nonsense! Besides, why shouldn't he take bribes? That's the way he was brought up, and everybody does it. But what a kind, pleasant face and how he smiles as he looks at me."

Pierre went to Princess Mary's to dinner.

As he drove through the streets past the houses that had been burned down, he was surprised by the beauty of those ruins. The picturesqueness of the chimney stacks and tumble-down walls of the burned-out quarters of the town, stretching out and concealing one another, reminded him of the Rhine and the Colosseum. The cabmen he met and their passengers, the carpenters cutting the timber for new houses with axes, the women hawkers, and the shopkeepers, all looked at him with cheerful beaming eyes that seemed to say: "Ah, there he is! Let's see what will come of it!"

At the entrance to Princess Mary's house Pierre felt doubtful whether he had really been there the night before and really seen Natásha and talked to her. "Perhaps I imagined it; perhaps I shall go in and find no one there." But he had hardly entered the room before he felt her presence with his whole being by the loss of his sense of freedom. She was in the same black dress with soft folds and her hair was done the same way as the day before, yet she was quite different. Had she been like this when he entered the day before he could not for a moment have failed to recognize her.

She was as he had known her almost as a child and later on as Prince Andrew's fiancée. A bright questioning light shone in her eyes, and on her face was a friendly and strangely roguish expression.

Pierre dined with them and would have spent the whole evening there, but Princess Mary was going to vespers and Pierre left the house with her.

Next day he came early, dined, and stayed the whole evening. Though Princess Mary and Natásha were evidently glad to see their visitor and though all Pierre's interest was now centered in that house, by the evening they had talked over everything and the conversation passed from one trivial topic to another and repeatedly broke off. He stayed so long that Princess Mary and Natásha exchanged glances, evidently wondering when he would go. Pierre noticed this but could not go. He felt uneasy and embarrassed, but sat on because he simply could not get up and take his leave.

Princess Mary, foreseeing no end to this, rose first, and complaining of a headache began to say good night.

"So you are going to Petersburg tomorrow?" she asked.

"No, I am not going," Pierre replied hastily, in a surprised tone and as though offended. "Yes... no... to Petersburg? Tomorrow—but I won't say good-by yet. I will call round in case you have any commissions for me," said he, standing before Princess Mary and turning red, but not taking his departure.

Natásha gave him her hand and went out. Princess Mary on the other hand instead of going away sank into an armchair, and looked sternly and intently at him with her deep, radiant eyes. The weariness she had plainly shown before had now quite passed off. With a deep and long-drawn sigh she seemed to be prepared for a lengthy talk.

When Natásha left the room Pierre's confusion and awkwardness immediately vanished and were replaced by eager excitement. He quickly moved an armchair toward Princess Mary.

"Yes, I wanted to tell you," said he, answering her look as if she had spoken. "Princess, help me! What am I to do? Can I hope? Princess, my dear friend, listen! I know it all. I know I am not worthy of her, I know it's impossible to speak of it now. But I want to be a brother to her. No, not that, I don't, I can't..."

He paused and rubbed his face and eyes with his hands.

"Well," he went on with an evident effort at self-control and coherence. "I don't know when I began to love her, but I have loved her and her alone all my life, and I love her so that I cannot imagine life without her. I cannot propose to her at present, but the thought that perhaps she might someday be my wife and that I may be missing that possibility... that possibility... is terrible. Tell me, can I hope? Tell me what I am to do, dear princess!" he added after a pause, and touched her hand as she did not reply.

"I am thinking of what you have told me," answered Princess Mary. "This is what I will say. You are right that to speak to her of love at present..."

Princess Mary stopped. She was going to say that to speak of love was impossible, but she stopped because she had seen by the sudden change in Natásha two days before that she would not only not be hurt if Pierre spoke of his love, but that it was the very thing she wished for.

"To speak to her now wouldn't do," said the princess all the same.

"But what am I to do?"

"Leave it to me," said Princess Mary. "I know..."

Pierre was looking into Princess Mary's eyes.

"Well?... Well?..." he said.

"I know that she loves... will love you," Princess Mary corrected herself.

Before her words were out, Pierre had sprung up and with a frightened expression seized Princess Mary's hand.

"What makes you think so? You think I may hope? You think...?"

"Yes, I think so," said Princess Mary with a smile. "Write to her parents, and leave it to me. I will tell her when I can. I wish it to happen and my heart tells me it will."

"No, it cannot be! How happy I am! But it can't be.... How happy I am! No, it can't be!" Pierre kept saying as he kissed Princess Mary's hands.

"Go to Petersburg, that will be best. And I will write to you," she said.

"To Petersburg? Go there? Very well, I'll go. But I may come again tomorrow?"

Next day Pierre came to say good-by. Natásha was less animated than she had been the day before; but that day as he looked at her

Pierre sometimes felt as if he was vanishing and that neither he nor she existed any longer, that nothing existed but happiness. "Is it possible? No, it can't be," he told himself at every look, gesture, and word that filled his soul with joy.

When on saying good-by he took her thin, slender hand, he could not help holding it a little longer in his own.

"Is it possible that this hand, that face, those eyes, all this treasure of feminine charm so strange to me now, is it possible that it will one day be mine forever, as familiar to me as I am to myself?... No, that's impossible!..."

"Good-by, Count," she said aloud. "I shall look forward very much to your return," she added in a whisper.

And these simple words, her look, and the expression on her face which accompanied them, formed for two months the subject of inexhaustible memories, interpretations, and happy meditations for Pierre. "'I shall look forward very much to your return....' Yes, yes, how did she say it? Yes, 'I shall look forward very much to your return.' Oh, how happy I am! What is happening to me? How happy I am!" said Pierre to himself.

CHAPTER XIX

There was nothing in Pierre's soul now at all like what had troubled it during his courtship of Hélène.

He did not repeat to himself with a sickening feeling of shame the words he had spoken, or say: "Oh, why did I not say that?" and, "Whatever made me say *'Je vousaime'*?" On the contrary, he now repeated in imagination every word that he or Natásha had spoken and pictured every detail of her face and smile, and did not wish to diminish or add anything, but only to repeat it again and again. There was now not a shadow of doubt in his mind as to whether what he had undertaken was right or wrong. Only one terrible doubt sometimes crossed his mind: "Wasn't it all a dream? Isn't Princess Mary mistaken? Am I not too conceited and self-confident? I believe all this—and suddenly Princess Mary will tell her, and she will be sure to smile and say: 'How strange! He must be deluding himself. Doesn't he know that he is a man, just a man, while I...? I am something altogether different and higher.'"

That was the only doubt often troubling Pierre. He did not now make any plans. The happiness before him appeared so inconceivable that if only he could attain it, it would be the end of all things. Everything ended with that.

A joyful, unexpected frenzy, of which he had thought himself incapable, possessed him. The whole meaning of life—not for him alone but for the whole world—seemed to him centered in his love and the possibility of being loved by her. At times everybody seemed to him to be occupied with one thing only—his future happiness. Sometimes it seemed to him that other people were all as pleased as he was himself and merely tried to hide that pleasure by pretending to be busy with other interests. In every word and gesture he saw allusions to his happiness. He often surprised those he met by his significantly happy looks and smiles which seemed to express a secret understanding between him and them. And when he realized that people might not be aware of his happiness, he pitied them with his whole heart and felt a desire somehow to explain to them that all that occupied them was a mere frivolous trifle unworthy of attention.

When it was suggested to him that he should enter the civil service, or when the war or any general political affairs were discussed on the assumption that everybody's welfare depended on this or that issue of events, he would listen with a mild and pitying smile and surprise people by his strange comments. But at this time he saw everybody—both those who, as he imagined, understood the real meaning of life (that is, what he was feeling) and those unfortunates who evidently did not understand it—in the bright light of the emotion that shone within himself, and at once without any effort saw in everyone he met everything that was good and worthy of being loved.

When dealing with the affairs and papers of his dead wife, her memory aroused in him no feeling but pity that she had not known the bliss he now knew. Prince Vasíli, who having obtained a new post and some fresh decorations was particularly proud at this time, seemed to him a pathetic, kindly old man much to be pitied.

Often in afterlife Pierre recalled this period of blissful insanity. All the views he formed of men and circumstances at this time remained true for him always. He not only did not renounce them subsequently, but when he was in doubt or inwardly at variance, he referred to the views he had held at this time of his madness and they always proved correct.

"I may have appeared strange and queer then," he thought, "but I was not so mad as I seemed. On the contrary I was then wiser and had more insight than at any other time, and understood all that is worth understanding in life, because... because I was happy."

Pierre's insanity consisted in not waiting, as he used to do, to discover personal attributes which he termed "good qualities" in people before loving them; his heart was now overflowing with love, and by loving people without cause he discovered indubitable causes for loving them.

CHAPTER XX

After Pierre's departure that first evening, when Natásha had said to Princess Mary with a gaily mocking smile: "He looks just, yes, just as if he had come out of a Russian bath—in a short coat and with his hair cropped," something hidden and unknown to herself, but irrepressible, awoke in Natásha's soul.

Everything: her face, walk, look, and voice, was suddenly altered. To her own surprise a power of life and hope of happiness rose to the surface and demanded satisfaction. From that evening she seemed to have forgotten all that had happened to her. She no longer complained of her position, did not say a word about the past, and no longer feared to make happy plans for the future. She spoke little of Pierre, but when Princess Mary mentioned him a long-extinguished light once more kindled in her eyes and her lips curved with a strange smile.

The change that took place in Natásha at first surprised Princess Mary; but when she understood its meaning it grieved her. "Can she have loved my brother so little as to be able to forget him so soon?" she thought when she reflected on the change. But when she was with Natásha she was not vexed with her and did not reproach her. The reawakened power of life that had seized Natásha was so evidently irrepressible and unexpected by her that in her presence Princess Mary felt that she had no right to reproach her even in her heart.

Natásha gave herself up so fully and frankly to this new feeling that she did not try to hide the fact that she was no longer sad, but bright and cheerful.

When Princess Mary returned to her room after her nocturnal talk with Pierre, Natásha met her on the threshold.

"He has spoken? Yes? He has spoken?" she repeated.

And a joyful yet pathetic expression which seemed to beg forgiveness for her joy settled on Natásha's face.

"I wanted to listen at the door, but I knew you would tell me."

Understandable and touching as the look with which Natásha gazed at her seemed to Princess Mary, and sorry as she was to see her agitation, these words pained her for a moment. She remembered her brother and his love.

"But what's to be done? She can't help it," thought the princess.

And with a sad and rather stern look she told Natásha all that Pierre had said. On hearing that he was going to Petersburg Natásha was astounded.

"To Petersburg!" she repeated as if unable to understand.

But noticing the grieved expression on Princess Mary's face she guessed the reason of that sadness and suddenly began to cry.

"Mary," said she, "tell me what I should do! I am afraid of being bad. Whatever you tell me, I will do. Tell me...."

"You love him?"

"Yes," whispered Natásha.

"Then why are you crying? I am happy for your sake," said Princess Mary, who because of those tears quite forgave Natásha's joy.

"It won't be just yet—someday. Think what fun it will be when I am his wife and you marry Nicholas!"

"Natásha, I have asked you not to speak of that. Let us talk about you."

They were silent awhile.

"But why go to Petersburg?" Natásha suddenly asked, and hastily replied to her own question. "But no, no, he must... Yes, Mary, He must...."